About the Author

A curious mind, an adventurous spirit and ever creative, R.J. Wilhelm has been writing for as long as he can remember. As the years have gone by, writing has become his escape from the responsibilities of adult life as his varied experiences lead to ever greater creativity and he identifies the sublime and absurd amongst the seemingly benign. When he isn't writing, you'll predominantly find him failing at parenthood, lamenting the corporate career he eschewed his sporting prowess for, running marathons, climbing mountains, touring England's finest watering holes, and travelling to as many corners of the world as possible with what little time remains.

Intimate and Explosive Adventures

A series of sensual and seductive short stories about one woman's search for satisfaction.

R. J. Wilhelm

Intimate and Explosive Adventures

*A series of sensual and seductive short stories about
one woman's search for satisfaction.*

Chimera

CHIMERA PAPERBACK

© Copyright 2024
R. J. Wilhelm

A CIP catalogue record for this title is
available from the British Library.

ISBN 978 1 915451 00 2

Chimera is an imprint of
Pegasus Elliot Mackenzie Publishers Ltd.
www.pegasuspublishers.com

First Published in 2024

Chimera
Sheraton House Castle Park
Cambridge England

Printed & Bound in Great Britain

To all the women that never had the opportunity to explore their sexuality.

Christmas Day (1)

It's the morning of Christmas Day. You and your man are tucked up naked in bed in the middle of the vast bedroom of the luxuriant Swiss chalet you're staying in. He's woken up but you're still asleep. He's lying there looking at you. You look so beautiful and peaceful. But he's also so attracted to and aroused by what he's looking at, he just can't control his desire to do something – anything – to you.

After fighting his desire for a while so as to let you sleep longer, eventually he can't hold back any more and he decides to wake you up with your first Christmas present. Stealthily, desperate not to disturb you too soon, he shuffles his body down the bed until right at the foot of it before turning onto his front and sliding back up the bed between your legs, which fortunately are spread sufficiently to allow him to sneak between them without you noticing.

When his head reaches your groin, he pauses to see if you stir from the feel of his breath on you. You continue to lay there, motionless. He waits a little longer and then, ever so softly and slowly, he starts to kiss your pussy.

He kisses it several times before you stir. You open your eyes and look around, a little confused, before noticing the sensation of his lips on your pussy for the first time. You look down to where he is to find him looking straight back up at you with as much of a naughty smile as he can muster while continuing to kiss you. Now comprehending what's going on, you let a little smile appear across your face and then allow yourself to relax into what you've woken up to.

For a while you maintain eye contact as he continues the initial gentle stimulation but, with you now awake and embracing the experience, it's not long before he redirects his gaze to your pussy to focus on upping the ante of his oral antics.

He presses his tongue up against it, trying to cover as much as your pussy as he can with warm moisture. He lets his tongue linger for a while to allow you to get used to feeling it up against you. Then he starts sliding his tongue all around your pussy, taking care to ensure that every bit of it gets attention.

"Oh yeah," you whisper as you settle in to the oral treat you're getting. He carries on sliding as much of his tongue as he can all over your pussy for several minutes, every now and then contorting it so as to give each part a different sensation.

Eventually, he notices his saliva being joined by fluid from your vagina. It's exactly what he'd been hoping for. Tasting this, he starts to increase the share of attention your clit gets. As he does so, your body starts to writhe around and you start to moan with pleasure.

Feeling, seeing and hearing this, he speeds up the pace with which his tongue slides over you. Your moans get louder and more frequent. He speeds up again and starts to focus more fully on your clit. Your body is now writhing around uncontrollably and he has to grab your buttocks firmly to keep you still enough for his tongue to stay on its intended target.

As he continues to pleasure you with his tongue while wrestling to keep your body suitably still, he realises the nascent proximity of his hands to some of your erogenous zones presents an opportunity. He sneaks the little finger of his right hand up to the opening of your ass. He starts stroking the opening in a circular motion.

As you feel this, your moans get louder and more frequent still. Hearing this, he penetrates your ass with his finger. "Ohhhh," you shout as he does so. Your moans turn to screams. He speeds up the pace of his oral stimulation a little further and starts slowly thrusting his little finger in and out of your ass, with his hands still clasped firmly against your buttocks. This thrusting into your ass sends you over the edge. You let out an almighty scream that seems to last for an eternity as you climax.

When the screaming stops and your body falls still, he lingers a little longer where he is before, delighted at the outcome of his efforts, he slides himself away from you and gets up. While you remain lying still, eyes closed in post-orgasmic elation, he opens the blinds on one side of the room to reveal the beautiful snowy mountain vista outside through the floor-to-ceiling bi-fold doors.

He then walks out of the room briefly before returning to the bedroom with two champagne flutes and a bucket filled with ice and a bottle of Bucks Fizz. He places it down next to the bed where you're still lying, a beautiful motionless vision. He gets back into bed and then grabs a small present from the top drawer of the bedside table. He snuggles up against you and places the small gift box on your abdomen. Feeling this, you open your eyes and look down at it, then at him.

"Just something a little silly," he says, looking back at you, just admiring the wonderful sight of you, naked in post-climactic bliss next to him.

Curious, you look back at the gift and then proceed to open it. Inside is a sexy silk red bra and panties set. You lift them out and hold them up. You see that the bra has holes around the nipples but is otherwise plain, while the panties say 'Ho Ho Ho' in white writing, with a hole strategically placed between each of the Os.

A little smile emerges across your face and you look at him. There's then a pause while your eyes meet. You're clearly thinking about something but he has no idea what. Eventually, to his surprise you break eye contact to sit up and put the bra and panties on. You then hop up and straddle him.

You don't say a word and just stare at him with a naughty look in your eyes. Holding your gaze, you start stroking your nipples through the holes in your bra. You carry on like this for about thirty seconds until you notice his cock, fully erect, pointing up at you out of the corner of your eye. You clasp it with your hand and start slowly stroking it.

Then you move your head down towards his groin, still looking him in the eyes, and softly kiss the tip of his cock. You keep stroking it and kiss it a few more times, pausing between each as you wait to see his reaction to the sensation.

Then you stop stroking and kissing it, leave your mouth lingering millimetres away and, still looking up at him, say, "Which hole do you want to put this in?"

He's once again caught off guard by this and a little unsure how to respond but after a very brief pause he can't help but go for broke so he smiles, raises his eyebrows and, half-answering, half-questioning, cheekily replies "All of them?"

You say nothing and instead, after a couple of seconds, open your mouth and wrap it around his cock, with your eyes still looking up at him. He lets out a moan of pleasure as you do so. You start sucking him and don't waste any time building up the intensity.

Your fellating feels fantastic. It's not long before you hear him frequently intersperse breathless whispers of "Oh yeah" and groans of pleasure. He can tell that if you carry on like this he's going to orgasm in no time but, realising this yourself from his reaction and the pre-cum now seeping into your mouth, you suddenly stop and lift your mouth off and away from his cock.

There's a silent pause for a few seconds as you stare into each other's eyes, in his case wondering what you might do next. Holding his gaze again, you lift your head away and then lift your body back on top of him.

Keeping your panties on, you lower yourself on to his rock-hard cock through the dedicated vaginal hole. He lets out a gasp of pleasure as you ingest him and he feels your soaking wet vagina. You start riding him, keeping your eyes fixated on him as you do so.

Again, you waste no time in picking up the pace and intensity. He starts groaning again as you do so. He's in heaven and never wants this to stop. Once again, he can feel he's going to cum in no time if you continue like this.

But after a couple of minutes of you riding him like this you suddenly stop once again, as if able to feel that he could climax any second. You say nothing and initially just stay where you are. But then you lift off him, turn around and get down on all fours so you're facing the beautiful mountain scene outside and your ass (and the asshole in your sexy new panties) is facing towards him. You then turn your head around to look at him, wiggle your butt at him a little and seductively whisper "Merry Christmas baby" to let him know this is his cue to take over.

Realising this, he abruptly sits up and proceeds to manoeuvre himself up behind you. You feel his rock-hard penis, covered in your juices, press up against your ass. He slowly slides it in. You let out a quiet "Mmm" as you feel your tight ass being filled.

He starts thrusting into you, slowly and gently at first to see how your respond. You let out a few quiet moans and a louder, "Oh yeah, fuck my ass," which let him know you're enjoying it. He speeds up his thrusting a little. It feels divine and once again he can tell if he carries on like this it's not going to be long before he cums, predominantly due to all the amazing hand-based, oral and vaginal stimulation you've already given him but as now augmented by your naughty titillation and the feel of your tight ass.

He's realised by now that you're doing all this for his pleasure rather than for you, as if to repay the oral awakening he gave you. But he can't resist wanting to please you too. So he ceases thrusting briefly, lowers his upper body to your back and gently pushes your hips down until you're laid flat on your front and he's laid on top of you. He recommences thrusting into your ass.

"You like this? You like having my hard dick in your ass?" he mumbles into your ear.

"Oh yeah," you reply.

"Would you like to have even more fun?" he continues.

"Oh yeah," you repeat.

After a few more thrusts into your ass, he then reaches his hands around and underneath you until they reach the front of your panties. Two of the fingers on his right hand find the strategically-placed clitoris hole and start stroking. You let out another moan, louder this time, as you feel this whilst taking his cock in your ass. Then two of the fingers on his left hand find the strategically-placed vagina hole and slide into your vagina. You let another moan as he does this, louder again.

"You like this?" he says again.

"Yes," you half-moan, half-say in reply.

You notice his breath on the back of your neck and ears, and then he starts kissing these areas whilst simultaneously thrusting into you, stroking your clit and finger-fucking your vagina. You start to moan more frequently. This in turn makes his cock start to throb.

"Oh yeah," he groans into your ear. You can feel his cock throbbing in your ass as it thrusts into you. You can tell he's so close to orgasm now. The combination of your prior stimulation, having your hot naked body at his behest, feeling your soft skin up against his, breathing in your intoxicating scent, tasting you with his lips, hearing you moan with pleasure and the feeling of your tight ass is out of this world.

Meanwhile, the combination of the feeling of submission under the weight of his body pressed on top of yours, hearing him groan and talk dirty regularly into your ear, feeling his breath on you, lips up against you, cock penetrating your ass and fingers stimulating your clit and vagina, and knowing that he's so close to orgasm because of you is turning you on as well.

Your body starts to writhe around a little, restricted though it is by having him on top of you, and you start to moan more frequently and more loudly. Every groan of his, a little louder each time, right into your ear is met by a moan back from you. Your body writhing around and your moans tell him you're loving this too.

"I'm going to cum," he grunts into your ear.

"Oh yeah, cum in me – cum in my ass," you moan back.

Hearing this, as well as hearing, seeing and feeling you get pleasure too sends him over the edge. He lets out a huge roar into your ear as he climaxes and starts to ejaculate into your ass. Hearing and feeling his explosion tips you over the edge: With him still roaring into your ear, you start screaming back as your body convulses with ecstasy and your vagina and ass tense around his fingers and cock.

Your orgasms eventually subside. He just lays there on top of you, his penis still in your ass. There's Bucks Fizz waiting to be consumed and a mountain full of adventure staring at you but he doesn't want to go anywhere; he just wants to stay inside of you with the soft skin of your hot body pressed up against his.

Repeating you from a few minutes earlier, but in a less naughty tone, he breathlessly says, "Happy Christmas, baby."

Christmas Day (2)

After lying there, your bodies entwined, for what feels like an age, he withdraws from you and rolls on to his side. You turn over and nestle your body back up against his. Again, you just lie there, gazing into each other's eyes with a mutually satisfied smile on your faces and softly stroking each other's buzzing bodies.

Eventually, you break the post-coital bliss by getting up and walking over to the bi-fold doors. You stand there gazing out to the glorious mountain view, the thick snow glistening in the morning sunshine. He continues to lie there, enjoying a glorious view of a different kind – your gorgeous naked body stood in front of him, with the sexy derriere he's just been riding looking back at him.

You turn and come back to the bed. You grab the Bucks Fizz from the bucket, pop the cork, half-fill the two flutes, get back on to the bed with a flute in each hand and pass him one. You cuddle up facing the alpine vista, one arm around each other and one holding the flute of Bucks Fizz.

You lay there consuming the Bucks Fizz for a little while longer. Then, a little reluctantly, you decide you should do something else as the morning is almost over already. You finally take your new bra and panties off and put the flutes down on the bedside tables. Then you get up and take his hand as you walk to the bathroom.

The bathroom is massive, with heated slate tile flooring, a large marble sink and a shower encased in glass that fills at least a quarter of the room. You open the door into the shower, walk on in with him behind you, still holding your hand. He closes the door behind you and you turn the shower on.

Not only is there a big rainwater shower head in the middle of the shower but there are also jets on the two walls in the corner. He doesn't want to wash you off him but the soothing hot water alleviates his disappointment.

Steam quickly starts to fill the room and you embrace under the rainwater shower, with the two jets spraying you from the side. Your bodies pressed up against each other and arms around each other, you kiss sensually as the water lashes against your skin.

You continue like this but start gently fondling each other's bodies with your hands. This continues for several minutes. The combination of the bodily contact and hot water lashing against you is arousing you once again.

Still kissing and your bodies up against each other, you move your hands towards his groin. They start stroking his testicles and then his penis. You carry on stroking him like this, initially very lightly but with increasing pressure.

His cock starts to harden. You feel this but, instead of waiting for it to get harder still in your hands, you stop kissing him and kneel down in front of him. With the water pounding you from several angles, you start sucking his cock. Very quickly, the sucking makes him fully erect.

It's not immediately apparent from the way you're behaving, other than the stimulation you're giving him, but you're very aroused again. Again, you don't wait around and, once you feel that he's fully erect in your mouth, you only continue sucking him for a few seconds longer. Then you remove his erection from your mouth, stand up, walk over to one of the walls and press your body up against it, placing your hands above you as you do so to make it clear that you want him to do you up against the wall from behind.

He follows you away from underneath the rainwater shower and places himself behind you. He's pleasantly surprised to find your vagina is flooded once again, not with shower water but rather the juices of your arousal. His hard cock easily slides into you as a result. You let out a moan as you feel him penetrate you.

The angle is such that he's immediately deep inside of you. The sensation is intense for both of you as a result. He places his hands on top of yours up above your head against the wall and begins thrusting into you.

The combination of the deep penetration, the feeling of submission of having him fuck you up against the wall and the water from the jets spraying all over you is really arousing you. Very quickly, you're moaning on a regular basis. You hear him groaning back at you, the feeling of being deep inside you and able to dominate you like this giving him such intense pleasure.

He continues fucking you like this, bit-by-bit getting harder and faster, for several minutes. Your moans and groans continue the whole time and neither of you want to stop. But, whilst he's loving it and can tell you're enjoying it too, he can tell that neither of you are going to orgasm like this – in his case because, whilst the pleasure is incredible, it's simply too soon after you last made him cum.

He slows down his thrusting to a standstill and withdraws from you. You turn around, you put your arms around each other and you start kissing once again. Then eventually you pull away from your embrace and, for the first time since entering the shower, turn your focus to cleaning yourselves.

Once suitably clean, you turn off the shower and you both exit through the glass door. Instead of wrapping yourselves in the towels provided, you hand him one of the white dressing gowns that's hanging on the back of the bathroom door and wrap the other around yourself. Still soaking wet but wrapped in your gowns, you walk through to the kitchen.

You both agree that you should belatedly start cooking the meal you'd planned in advance as it's going to take a long time. Still in your dressing gowns, you set about making it, you taking care of the dishes you've agreed to take responsibility for and him likewise for the dishes he's agreed to prepare.

Again, the kitchen – actually a double-aspect kitchen-diner – is large and luxuriant, with big marble surfaces, a vast array of cooking utensils and floor-to-ceiling windows at either end showing off once again the beautiful mountain scenery surrounding the chalet.

You put some music on and both start preparing the food, chatting, laughing and drinking more of the Bucks Fizz as you go. After about half an hour, all of your dishes are fully prepared and you pop them in the oven. He's still busy working on his but, with nothing else to do for a while as you wait for your dishes to cook and him to finish with his, your mind starts to wonder.

As he stands against one of the large surfaces, continuing to mix ingredients, you walk over to him and put your arms around him from behind. He keeps mixing. Initially, you just hold him but then he feels your lips against the back of his neck and your hands start to wander.

As you continue to kiss his neck, your hands start slowly stroking his chest before descending down over his abdomen until they reach the knot where he's tied the gown. He hasn't tied tightly and, as your hands continue moving lower, you simultaneously loosen the knot and his gown falls open. You stop kissing him briefly and, pretending it was an accident but both of you knowing it was anything but, you say "Oops, how did that happen?"

There now being no barrier to his body, your hands move off the dressing gown and on to his newly-revealed skin. Initially, you move them up and stroke his previously-covered chest, but then you slide them back down again, meandering from side to side somewhat, across his abdomen and to the top of his legs. You brush his testicles as you move to stroke the inside of his legs and thighs. You keep stroking the inside of his legs and thighs, deliberately brushing his testicles every now and again, with increasing frequency, and latterly brushing the tip of his penis as well.

Whilst continuing to stroke around the top of his legs with one hand, you grab his cock in your other and start to tug on it. You find that it's already pretty hard from all your titillation but the feel of your hand wrapped around it and the jerking action very quickly stiffens it to the point of being rock solid.

He's now long since stopped preparing food and just stands there letting himself indulge in the pleasure you're giving him. You continue kissing his neck whilst tugging his now-seriously solid cock. Then you take the other hand that's been continuing to stroke his inside leg and thighs, grab as much of his balls as you can and start stroking them.

Continuing to kiss him and now stroking his testicles, you pick up the pace and intensity of your tugging. The combination of stimulation feels divine. You start interspersing your kissing with whispering dirty talk into his ear: "How does that feel baby? You like it when I jerk you off? You like it when I stroke your cock? Does this make you want to explode?" He's so aroused by the dirty talk that it makes his cock throb. You feel this as you're tugging him. "Ooh you do like this, don't you baby?" you continue, exciting him even more.

Even though you could make him orgasm imminently if you carry on like this, you stop kissing him and whispering in his ear, shuffle away from him and then pull on his side to turn him around, away from the worktop and the ingredients situated on top. You see his half-uncovered body through his dressing gown and an erection pointing directly at you. Once again, you kneel down in front of him and start fellating him.

He has no idea what he's done to deserve all the oral pleasure you're giving him today but he decides that it's not fair that you're doing so much for him without getting anything in return. Not that he wants to – your blow-job technique feels incredible – but he pulls his cock out of your mouth and grabs your hands so as to pull you back up.

There's a brief pause as you look into each other's eyes, you now unsure what he's going to do next. He then picks you up and carries you over to the now-empty marble surface you'd previously been preparing your dishes on, lays you down on it, and gets on it on top of you but facing away from you so that his cock is dangled above your face and his face hovers about 6 inches above your pussy.

He undoes your dressing gown to reveal your pussy and, after all the stimulation you've given him, he wastes no time in taking a mouthful of it. The way you've been sucking him has made him want to eat you so much.

As you feel the warm moisture of his mouth over your pussy, you open your mouth and re-ingest his hard dick into it. He slides his tongue all over your pussy; he wants to taste all of it. You start sucking his cock again. He starts groaning with pleasure into your pussy as you do so. Feeling the vibration of this adds to your stimulation and you let out a muffled moan into his cock. This in turn causes him to groan again, louder this time, which in turn provides a more intense vibration for you and again causes you to moan back into his cock.

This virtuous circle of stimulation is turning you both on so much. Hearing you start to moan more and more frequently and loudly whilst you suck him lets him know you're thoroughly enjoying this. He increasingly focusses his oral stimulation on your clitoris and then, as he notices your juices start to seep from your vagina, decides to insert two fingers from his right hand into you. Continuing to lick your clit, he reaches his fingers as far inside you as he can and begins to stroke the inner walls of your vagina.

It takes you a little by surprise at first but after a few seconds of adjustment, he feels you relax and he notices your moans go to a new level. You're now virtually screaming into his cock. Feeling his fingers inside you, you decide to start using your hands once again, placing one on his shaft and the other back on his testicles. Continuing to fellate him, you begin to stroke his balls once again and tug on his shaft.

The combination of all of this and the vibration of your screams, all while he can see, feel and hear you enjoying yourself, takes things to another level for him.

His cock starts to throb so much it's clear he's going to orgasm any moment.

But he doesn't want to climax without you so, whilst continuing to lick you out and caress your vagina, he quickly contemplates how he might be able to bring you with him. He opts to insert a finger from his spare hand into your ass and start thrusting into you with it.

Thankfully, his gamble pays off – adding to the clitoral and vaginal stimulation, and the vibration of his now-very loud moans, the anal penetration takes you over the edge: Unable to control himself, just as he erupts, so do you.

The pleasure for you is so great that as you climax you have to remove your mouth from his cock to let out an enormous scream. But, feeling and hearing him explode at the same time, you somehow manage to continue jerking him off and his spunk flies into your mouth as you scream. Your respective orgasms are so intense and seem to go on that much longer because of the simultaneousness, each being prolonged by hearing and feeling the other's.

Eventually, your ecstasy dissipates. He uses your legs to slump his head onto and you let go of his cock and balls, turn your head to one side and just let his softening penis flop against your neck as you let out a satisfied sigh.

But then your post-orgasmic rapture is rudely interrupted when the alarm on the oven starts going off. It's time for you to check on one of your dishes. Too rapidly for his liking, he peels himself off you, then you both hop off the worktop and stand up before returning to your respective dishes, almost as if nothing's happened.

Christmas Day (3)

It's almost mid-afternoon by the time you sit down to eat. What you've made tastes sublime – the best thing he's tasted since your pussy a short while earlier – and his contributions aren't too shabby either.

After the day's activities so far, and how long it took to prepare, you're both now feeling pretty ravenous; after all the hard work, the food is gone in a flash. The upside of this is it gives you both more time to do other things. Having had the Swiss mountains as the backdrop to most of today's activities, now feeling re-energised, you decide to take a walk.

You both wrap up warm and venture out into the snow. The sunshine has been covered by cloud now but it's calm outside. You don't have any particular plan on where to head so decide to walk in the vague direction of what looks to be the nearest peak.

It's not long, though, before you decide you want to play. Out of the blue, you bend down, grab a handful of snow and throw it at him from point-blank range. The left side of his face gets covered. Quickly getting over the shock, he bends down and picks up his own handful of snow. But by the time he's stood up, you've started running away. He starts chasing after you and eventually gets close enough to launch his handful of snow at you. Some of it collides with your back but in general it's a pretty poor show of retaliation.

Feeling the snow against the back of your coat, you realise he's now unarmed. You turn, see where he is and what he's up to and proceed to grab another handful of snow, this time taking some time to roll it into a proper ball. Seeing you preparing another missile like this, he does likewise. You launch your respective snowballs at each other and then set about making more.

This escalates into a few minutes of all-out snowball warfare. Although he has a stronger throw, your snowballs are of a far higher quality and make contact with their target with much greater regularity as a result.

After being routinely pelted by your superior snowballs for several minutes, he changes tack and runs towards you armed with as much snow as he can carry. You see him coming but instead of running away you stay and launch more (lower quality) balls at him as he approaches. He takes the hits and continues heading straight for you. You keep throwing but eventually he gets to you and unloads the snow he's carrying all over your face and upper body like a blizzard of semen at the end of a porn film.

You're temporarily blinded by the blanket of snow and he seizes the opportunity to tackle you to the ground. The ferocity with which he tackles you means you plug hard into the snow on impact. He lands on top of you and buries you ever so slightly further. You open your eyes, now cleansed of snow, and see his face a few inches above you, looking at you and grinning. He kisses you. You realise from this the war is over and kiss him back.

You lay there kissing in the snow for quite some time, but after a while you being wedged between him and the compacted snow becomes uncomfortable so he lifts off you and helps you up. Realising you're both quite cold now, you opt to walk back to the chalet.

On arrival, you take off your coats and head straight to the living room with its feature fireplace to warm up. He turns on the fire and you sit down on the large soft warming rug that's sat beside it. When you're feeling sufficiently warm again, you decide it's time for presents – proper presents, not the cheeky present he gave you in bed earlier in the day. You hand him yours and he hands you his. You open each other's gifts at the same time. It transpires you've both got each other one nice and one naughty gift. Both smiling when you see what you've received, you proceed to embrace and kiss once again.

With presents out the way, he heads over to the large mahogany drinks cabinet that stands elegantly in one corner of the living room. It's fabulously well-stocked. He pours himself a brandy and rustles up a cocktail for you. He brings them over and sets them down on the coffee table that sits in the middle of the room, next to the rug. Then he goes over to the other corner of the room where there's a stack of games. He brings a handful of them over and sets them down next to the drinks on the coffee table.

He hands you your drink and you each take a sip before he grabs one of the games.

As he opens it, he asks you "Which would you prefer: Loser has to perform a sexual favour of the other player's choosing or loser has to take a piece of clothing off?" Still thawing out a little, it not yet quite dark outside, and with the amount of sexual activity you've already shared today, you opt for the more sedate option. You start playing.

After an hour or so you've played all of the games he brought over and it's not gone particularly well for him; you're merely topless whereas he's now got nothing left on except his boxer shorts.

"Another one?" you ask with a smile, effectively asking if he wants to get naked.

By this stage, it's going so badly he decides he may as well continue so he says "Yes."

To both of your surprise, he wins this one – with a bit of good fortune – and you remove your trousers.

"Another?" you ask, just as you finish pulling them off.

"Sure," he replies, half-believing his luck may have changed.

But it hasn't. He loses and is forced to remove his boxer shorts. You watch him and smile as his penis reappears in front of you. Luckily, it's now completely dark outside, although you're in such a remote place the chance of anyone seeing in is extremely unlikely in any event.

"Time to do something else," he announces, there now being nothing left for him to remove if he loses again. He gets up and walks to the kitchen, before returning a couple of minutes later with a chocolate fondue machine. He sets it down next to the rug you've been playing on, plugs it in to the nearest plug point and turns it on.

You weren't expecting this but neither are you disappointed; the walk, snowball fight and games have given you a chance to work up your appetite for some dessert. After a couple of minutes letting the chocolate heat up, he feeds you a mouthful. You then reciprocate. He feeds you another mouthful. Again, you reciprocate. He then intimates he's going to feed you for a third time but at the last second surprises you by deviating the chocolate away from your mouth and letting it fall on to your breasts.

"Oops," he says, wholly insincerely. "I guess I'd better clean up the mess I made."

You let out a hint of a wry smile as he moves his head towards your breasts and starts to clean up the chocolate 'mess' with his mouth.

"Let me get you some more," he says once he's removed all the chocolate from your body. He again intimates that he's going to feed you but deviates just as you open your mouth to ingest it and he lets it drop onto your body once again. This time it lands on and around your nave.

"Oops," he repeats. "Let me clean that up again."

He moves his head down towards your nave and again cleans up the chocolate with his mouth. In the midst of doing so, he not-so-subtly takes the opportunity to pull down your thong.

Sitting up again, he grabs some more chocolate but this time, instead of initially pretending to feed you, he just throws it straight at you. He's taken a big load this time and it goes all over your upper body, as well as parts of your legs, arms and even the rug. Without asking, he starts cleaning up the chocolate with his mouth again. But this time, he takes things very slowly, lingering at each place the chocolate has landed. You feel his lips all over your upper body, and then down to the parts of your legs where the chocolate has landed. Once he thinks he's got it all, he heads back up towards your upper body but stops around your groin.

"I think I missed a bit," he says, looking up at you as he does so.

There's no chocolate there but that doesn't stop him from placing his mouth on your pussy. He kisses it and works his mouth all around it, softly and slowly. You let out a little moan. He stays there for a couple of minutes before lifting up and reaching for more chocolate. This time he flicks it directly towards your pussy. Most of the chocolate lands just around it rather than on it so he gets some more chocolate and flicks it towards your pussy again. More of it reaches its intended destination on this occasion and he follows it with his mouth.

He starts licking the warm chocolate from off your pussy. You let out another moan. When it's all gone, he carries on teasing your pussy with his tongue, working his way around it as if to make doubly sure he hasn't missed any.

This carries on for several minutes, during which your moans get more frequent. He starts to inhale an exhilarating odour from your vagina as juices start to emanate from it. This turns him on even more than he already is by you and he takes the decision, now that he's erect, to remove his tongue from your pussy.

You're somewhat stunned and open your eyes to see him shuffling up on top of you. You didn't really want him to stop but when you feel his erection up against you and realise he wants to have sex you acquiesce, relax and open your legs a little wider. Your eyes are fixated on one another as he enters you. He starts slowly thrusting in and out of you.

He continues like this for several minutes but then, surprising you once again, he withdraws and proceeds to flick another load of chocolate all over your body. You look at him, confused. Rather than licking the chocolate up or re-entering you, he goes back down on you. Your confusion and slight disappointment from his previous curtailment of oral stimulation turns to delight as you feel his tongue back on your pussy.

He continues eating you out for several minutes, all while your body's covered in chocolate. But then he stops and shuffles up on top of you once again. Again, you're left frustrated and have to 'settle' for having him inside you.

This time, with his hard cock back inside you, he lifts your legs up and rests your ankles on his shoulders. This allows him to thrust deeper inside you. He does so much harder and faster this time. In fact, it's not long before he's really pummelling you with his cock. The pounding you're taking and feeling his solid cock so deep inside you makes you gasp with every thrust.

But eventually, and quite abruptly, to your surprise he withdraws from you once again before reaching for the chocolate and flicking even more of it over you. You (and plenty of the rug but it's not your house so who cares?) are now completely covered in chocolate but he makes no attempt to eat it off you – except that which has landed back on your pussy.

He returns his mouth to your pussy and starts caressing it once again. You start moaning again but are also half-concerned he's going to frustrate you once more so initially don't embrace his oral stimulation. But after a few minutes it's clear he's not going anywhere this time and you let yourself relax.

He feels your body do so and starts to predominately focus his tongue titillation on your clit. Then he supplements this by lifting up his hands and starting to stroke your chocolate-covered breasts. After a couple of minutes of this, he lets his hands start sliding all over your body, wiping the chocolate as he goes.

You start moaning more frequently now. The heavenly oral stimulation accompanied by the warmth of the fire on your skin and his stroking of your chocolate-lathered body feels divine. Your body starts writhing around as he ups the intensity of his clitoral caressing. Your moans get louder, and you start interspersing shouts of "Yes. Yes. Yes." at regular intervals.

He continues like this, turned on even more by how much you're clearly enjoying it. Your body writhes around even more, almost uncontrollably now. Your moans and shouts get louder and more frequent still. And then you let out one long deafening scream as you reach orgasmic ecstasy.

When, eventually, you fall silent and your body falls motionless, he shuffles up on top of you once again and just lays there, watching you in your post-orgasmic wonderment. After a minute or so you open your eyes and see him looking back at you. There's a pause as you just stare into each other's eyes, your naked bodies stuck together with the chocolate.

Almost inconsequential as you lay there, you can feel his erection pressing up against you. But after a couple of minutes more of gazing into each other's eyes, without breaking your stare, you reach down and pull his penis towards the entrance of your vagina. You stop as the tip nudges up against you. You then put your hands on his buttocks and pull him towards you. He enters you, letting out a gasp as he does so. Still staring into each other's eyes, he starts ever so slowly thrusting into you.

He continues slowly thrusting into you, all the while staring into your eyes, for several minutes. There's no need for words as you can virtually read each other through your eyes, and the only sound is of you softly panting from the feeling of him penetrating you.

Then, completely out of the blue, you use all your strength to roll him over onto his back, you rolling with him as he goes. With you now lying on top of him, you take his arms and pin them to the floor above his head.

Next, with you both still staring into each other's eyes, you start slowly riding him. He lets out a groan as you start to do so; it feels wonderful but not quite as wonderful as knowing that you want to pleasure him like this.

You continue riding him, picking up the pace slightly. He starts to groan with pleasure more frequently. But he's not seeing any evidence that you're enjoying this – you're not panting any more, in particular – so he forces his hands free from your grasp and pushes your legs down, so you fall flat on top of him.

Your chocolate-covered bodies stick together once again. Then he grabs your buttocks with his chocolate-covered hands and pulls them towards him as he starts thrusting into you so as to grind his pubic bone up against your clit with each thrust. You're pleasantly surprised by this and let out a squeak as you feel your clit being stimulated like this while being penetrated.

Your face is only a matter of millimetres above him in this position but you're still staring into each other's eyes. He grabs your buttocks tighter, pulls them more firmly up against him and speeds up the speed and intensity of his thrusting into you. You both start moaning with pleasure. Seeing and hearing this turns you both on even more.

He keeps thrusting, getting harder and faster every few seconds, grinding up against your clit more intensely. Your mutual moaning picks up another notch, as the intensity of his thrusting into you builds further. As if the sound of your moaning didn't make it clear enough, you can see in each other's eyes the pleasure you're giving each other.

He thrusts in and out of you, harder and faster still. The constant grinding of your clit as he does so brings your moaning to a scream. He feels your chocolate-covered body tense up against his and he can tell you're close to orgasm.

He grabs your buttocks even more firmly and picks up the intensity of his thrusting further still. Your body starts to tremble. Feeling this, from nowhere he gets an urge to kiss you. He presses his lips up against yours and muffles the screams now emanating from your mouth.

Your body trembles more frenetically as his super-hard cock begins throbbing. His thrusting becomes even more furious. He clasps your buttocks even more tightly. With your lips still locked; your muffled screams are accompanied by his muffled grunts.

The amalgamation of dual stimulation of your vagina and clit, the feeling of closeness from having his lips and body pressed up against yours, the sense of submission from having his hands pressed so firmly against your buttocks and at giving into his choice of sexual antics, the naughtiness and sensation of chocolate strewn everywhere, the warmth of the fire on your skin and the knowledge that you're turning him on so much becomes too much: You fight your lips away from his to enable 'yourself to emit the almighty scream you have to as you orgasm. You've done him a favour as it allows him to roar straight back at you as his body is consumed with ecstasy and his throbbing cock begins to erupt into you at exactly the same time. Your mutual euphoria seems to last forever, and your mutual screaming and roaring continue just as long.

Finally, your orgasms subside and your head and body just fall limp on top of him. You lay there, nestled up against him. He moves his hands from their firm grasp of your buttocks and wraps them around you to hold you. You both just lay there blissfully, chocolate-covered bodies entwined, in front of the fire. Who knows what time it is now? Is it even Christmas Day still? Who cares? You've both had the most incredible day and you're ending it right where you want to be – in heaven, in the middle of nowhere, him inside you and you in his arms.

A Tripartite Triumph

You and your man find an evening where you can be together. You decide in advance that this is a night where you're going to try and have a threesome involving another man for the first time. You book an upmarket hotel and meet there in the early evening to check-in. You go and briefly survey the room and dump your excess baggage before heading back down to the bar adjacent to the hotel.

It's a sexy bar, spacious with a contrast between the low-level candle-lighting of the seating areas and the bright neon colours of the bar area itself. You take a seat at one of the tables. You both take in the scene for a moment before looking at the menu. A waiter comes over and takes your order – a passionfruit-led cocktail for you and an old-fashioned for him.

Whilst you wait for your drinks, you look around the bar to see who else is around. It's busy and there's a constant hum of talking and occasional laughing alongside the background chill-out music. Although the lighting is low, there's enough for you to make out everyone in the place. You slowly and subtly check out every guy in the bar.

After a couple of minutes, your surveying is interrupted by the arrival of the drinks. You clink your glasses together above the candle in the middle of your round table and say "Cheers," looking each other in the eye as you do so. It's the first word you've said, other than ordering your drinks, since checking into the hotel. There's an excited anticipation that means you don't know what to say.

You both take a sip and then he asks you if there's anyone that you like the look of. "Hmm, there were a couple of guys but I'm not sure they were quite what I was looking for," you reply. He asks you which ones to try and get an idea of what you might be looking for. You describe them and his eyes glance around the bar until he spots them. He pauses and absorbs what they look like, how they're dressed and what they're drinking. Then his eyes turn back to you and you both take another sip of your drinks, whilst looking into each other's eyes.

After a few seconds, your gaze is broken when you notice out of the corner of your eye a guy walking into the bar. He walks past your table and up to the bar itself, where he pitches up on one of the stools beside it.

Your man is now looking at this guy as he realises this is what distracted you. He looks back at you, where your eyes meet once again. You don't say a word, but rather just raise your eyebrows in a quizzical manner as if to say 'We've found our man. How about it?' He briefly pauses to contemplate before giving a gentle nod of agreement.

You take another sip of your drinks and he notices out of the corner of his eye that the man at the bar is now being handed a drink too. The guy takes a sip. You both sit there, silently, sipping your drinks on and off for a couple of minutes, clandestinely watching the man at the bar do likewise. You then take a deep breath, stand up and walk over slowly but confidently to the man at the bar.

"Hi," you say, a hint of a friendly smile appearing on your face as you do so.

"Hi," he replies, a friendly expression similarly appearing on his face as he does so.

"Would you like to have a threesome?" you continue, feeling particularly frisky and completely uninterested in making small talk.

The guy is taken aback but tries not to show it. Calmly, he looks at you and then around the bar where he sees your man looking back at him. Now comprehending the situation better, the man at the bar then looks back at you and says, "OK."

With a faint naughty-looking smile you say "Come with me." You grab his hand and drag him away from his stool towards your table, where you similarly grab your man's hand with your free hand and pull him up and away from his chair.

To avoid drawing too much attention to the three of you, you let go of their hands and walk ahead. They both follow close behind. You lead them to the hotel room. You open the door and then hold it open, gesturing them both in. You close the door behind them and walk towards the king-sized bed, once again taking one arm of each of theirs in yours.

You stop everyone next to the bed and take your dress off to reveal your sultry body and luxurious bright skimpy underwear. You turn to your man, look him in the eyes and unbutton his shirt, before proceeding to peel the shirt off him. You then turn to the other man and do exactly the same.

You then turn back to your man, look him in the eyes again and unzip the fly in his trousers, before peeling the trousers down and off him. As you do so, you reveal his boxer shorts with a solid bulge pointing through them at you. You notice it but don't react. Then you once again turn to the other man and take off his trousers in the same way. Again, you notice a bulge pointing through his underwear back at you.

You now have one guy stood either side of you in just their underwear with erect penises pointing at you. Standing between them, you start slowly stroking both bulges through the underwear at the same time, taking it in turns to look them in the eyes.

After a minute or so of this, when you feel both erections get harder, you stop and proceed to take their underwear off, your man first and then the man from the bar. You then kneel down so that their hard cocks are level with your face. You take one cock in each hand and start slowly tugging them, looking at their cocks in turn as you do this.

After a minute or two of this, you look up at your man and, whilst continuing to tug on both cocks, place your mouth around your man's and start gently sucking it, keeping your eyes focussed on his as you do it. He lets out a quiet groan of pleasure as you do so.

After a minute or two of this, you take your mouth away from his cock, turn to the other man and do the same (gently sucking his cock whilst looking up into his eyes and tugging on both of their cocks). Again, after a minute or two of this, you stop and remove his cock from your mouth. You then stand up and remove your underwear as if to say, "I'm ready for you boys." You climb on to the bed, stopping in the middle, where you wait on all fours facing away from both men. You then turn your head back to the two men and say seductively, "Who wants me first?"

Your man can see the moisture seeping out of your pussy in front of him and can't resist so hitches up behind you and inserts his rock-hard cock into you. You let out a slight moan of pleasure as he does so. He starts slowly thrusting in and out of you. You moan again.

After a brief period of you getting used to having him thrusting inside of you, you turn your head towards the other guy and firmly say "Come here." He walks around and stops in front of you. As your man continues to fuck you from behind, you take this guy's cock in your hand and start sucking it and tugging it again.

Everyone starts moaning – your man from the pleasure of fucking you, the stranger from the bar from the pleasure of you sucking and tugging him, and you from the pleasure of having two dicks inside you.

You all carry on like this for a while, revelling in the pleasure, but eventually you stop sucking and tugging the other guy and pull your body away from your man's cock. You stay on all fours but take your man's arm and pull him around and underneath you.

You're now face-to-face and, as you look into each other's eyes, you lower your body so as to take his now-throbbing cock back inside you. You move up and down a couple of times as if to make sure everything is exactly right before pausing and turning your head up to the other guy who's still in front of you (and now your man as well). "I want you in my ass," you say to him.

He duly obliges, walking around, positioning himself behind you and then attempting to penetrate your ass. Although his cock is wet from your sucking, he decides your ass isn't wet enough so he spits at it and then attempts once again to penetrate you, using the combination of your saliva on his cock and his saliva in and around your ass to facilitate matters.

This time he's successful and you feel his cock slide deep into your ass. You let out a big moan of pleasure as he does so. You now have two hard dicks deep inside you, one in your vagina and one in your ass. They both start thrusting in and out of you, with you sandwiched between them.

Your man stares into your eyes, which are just a few inches above him, as he fucks you. He sees you sometimes staring back at him, sometimes with your eyes closed and sometimes with your eyes rolling to the back of your head with pleasure.

Both guys thrust faster and harder into you. You start moaning repeatedly, getting louder all the time. They moan along with you – the pleasure of fucking your pussy and ass feels so good and seeing and hearing you get more and more aroused in turn arouses them more.

They continue to double-team you, harder and faster. You're now so wet your man can feel your juices dripping out of you. He can feel himself getting close to orgasm; the combination of the pleasure of fucking your pussy, feeling your naked body against his, feeling your juices drip onto him, seeing the pleasure in your eyes right above him, hearing the pleasure in what are now bordering on screams coming from your mouth, inhaling the combination of your natural scent, your perfume and the scent emanating from your soaking wet pussy, and feeling your breath on his face as you pant and scream is overwhelming.

But, even though it's clear you're thoroughly enjoying yourself, it doesn't seem to him as he looks into your eyes that you're going to climax. So, as they both continue to fuck you, he moves his hand towards your clitoris.

He starts stroking it and, as he does, you let out a full-on scream from the unexpected extra pleasure. He keeps stroking it and you keep screaming as he does so. This was all the extra stimulation you needed and it's not long before your body tenses and you let out an enormous scream as you have the most intense orgasm. Seeing, hearing and feeling you orgasm brings both guys to orgasm as well. With your orgasm ongoing, they let out roars of their own as they both ejaculate into you.

Eventually, your respective orgasms subside but you all just stay where you are, revelling in the post-coital bliss. Your man notices you open your eyes, which had closed during your orgasm. You look at him and a smile appears across your face.

You stay where you are for a little longer before the other guy removes his penis from your ass and you then lift off your man's cock. You get up with the intention of heading to the bathroom but, as you do, the other man says, "Wait, I want to see my cum in your ass."

You're a little surprised but, given how satisfied you're feeling, you accede to his request and proceed to get back onto all fours in the middle of the bed. Both men watch as a combination of their spunk and your pussy juices starts seeping out of both your vagina and ass all over the bed. You watch their faces as they watch the seeping of the juices.

When it feels like there's no more to come out, you ask him "Is there anything else you'd like?" with a naughty grin on your face. You ask it semi-rhetorically and head to the bathroom before he has a chance to answer, not that he knew what to say anyway.

The men put their clothes back on. As you come out of the bathroom, you see he's ready to go and so you go over to him, still naked, and say "Well, thank you for that. You gave me exactly what I wanted." With that, he opens the door and leaves the hotel, leaving you and your man in the room to digest the evening's events.

The Show

It's the evening of your very first burlesque show. You're backstage getting ready to perform, feeling both nervous and excited about putting everything you've learned about burlesque in your classes over the last few weeks into practice in equal measure. You put on your burlesque attire and accompanying make-up. Once complete, you give yourself a look in the mirror; you look absolutely ravishing. Seeing this causes you to relax and regain your confidence.

The call comes to let you know it's your turn to go and perform. You take a deep breath, give yourself a further final look in the mirror and head for the stage. You find a room full of people, eyes all fixated on you, on the edge of their seats in anticipation. You feel alive.

The music comes on and you get to work strutting your stuff. You absolutely nail your routine – every gyration of your body, every seductive wink or point at someone in the audience, every timely removal of a piece of clothing.

You look so enticing and do such a fabulous job with the seductive routine that, unbeknown to you, by the end of it there are several men in the audience that are totally aroused, desperately lusting for you with a full erection.

The fact that their significant other is in some cases sat right next to them changes nothing (although this makes them more uncomfortable as they try to conceal the bulge in their trousers) – you've driven them wild.

But there's one man in the audience who's twice as turned on by you by the end of your performance as everyone else. He knows you, knows what you're capable of, knows you're so much more than just a gorgeous girl who can take her clothes off, tease and flirt. He watches the start of the next act before subtly making his way out of the arena and backstage to where your dressing room is situated. After a big round of applause from the audience, you've returned to the dressing room to change your clothes, feeling liberated and ecstatic. He knocks on the dressing room door. One of your fellow acts opens it. "Hi," she says. "Can I help you?"

He asks if you're in there.

"Yes. I'll just get her for you," she answers.

She turns and walks out of sight into the dressing room. "There's someone waiting outside for you," he hears her say from a distance.

Perplexed, and not yet fully changed, you make your way to the door. You're shocked to see who's stood there waiting for you. "Oh my God, what are you doing here?" you ask as you see who it is. You hadn't spotted him in the audience while you were performing and had no idea he was there.

"Hey. I saw your performance and wanted to come and say congratulations. You were amazing out there," he answers.

"Thank you," you reply as a beaming smile appears across your face. There's then a short silence as you wait, expecting him to say something else. But he doesn't say anything, he just stands there looking at you. You have no idea but it's not that he doesn't want to say anything, he simply can't find the words. Eventually, to break the impasse, you say "Was there something else?"

He looks around, seemingly surveying the venue, before returning his gaze to you and says, "Have you got a few minutes?"

You check what time it is and then ponder briefly; you were planning on going to watch the rest of your newly trained troupe perform as soon as you were changed so this interruption has upset your plans somewhat. But, because it's him, you accept the diversion. "Sure," you reply.

With that, to your slight surprise he grabs your left hand with his right, turns and walks you down the corridor until you reach a door that says, 'Staff Only'. He stops outside it, looks around quickly and then opens the door, dragging you through it. He closes the door behind you and proceeds to lock it using the bolt that's situated halfway up it. You're a little uneasy about what's going on, being taken to a place that's clearly off limits and being locked in it alone with him.

You catch a glimpse of the room as you enter – it's relatively nondescript, an area of about seven square metres with white walls, faded blue carpets, a desk in one corner, a corner sofa in the other and nothing else of note – and then look at him as he turns towards you once he's finished locking the door.

There's another pause as he just stares at you, with an expression on his face that you can't quite put your finger on. He breaks the pause by quietly saying "You turned me on so much out there. I want to return the favour."

There's a very brief pause as you look at each other before he pounces on you – moving forward to within an inch of you, putting his hands on your cheeks, pulling them towards him and pressing his lips firmly against yours.

You realise as he does so that the expression on his face as he stared into your eyes was one of pure unadulterated desire. He kisses you passionately, moving his hands away from your cheeks and down your body to wrap them around your waist as he does so. He uses them to pull your body firmly up against his. As your bodies collide, you feel his erect cock up against your groin through your clothes. You realise just how aroused you have made him, how much he wants you.

As you haven't pushed him away, he feels validated to continue, so after about a minute of being passionately kissed like this, he shocks you by lifting you up, wrapping your legs around his body and carrying you over to the wall behind you, where he presses you up against it.

He proceeds to continue kissing you, but it's not too long before he moves from your lips to your neck. Here, he gets to smell your scent more clearly and he loves it, whispering "You smell divine," in your ear.

He continues kissing your neck for some time, occasionally switching to kiss and gently nibble on the edges of your ears as well. Being suspended in mid-air, pressed up against the wall with your legs around him, feeling his lips against you and hearing him whisper the occasional compliment in your ear feels good.

The initial shock wears off slightly and you start to feel disarmed. You've gone from feeling sexy at putting all of your femininity on show for a transfixed audience to feeling aroused from having one of them display his arousal and affection towards you like this.

Eventually, the skin on your neck isn't enough for him. He momentarily stops kissing you and carries you over to the desk, where he lays you down and climbs on top of you. He starts kissing your neck once again, whispering "You taste so good," in your ear as he does so, before moving his lips to the other areas of your body that currently have exposed skin – your arms.

He makes sure to kiss every last bit of them, going all the way to your hands, where he occasionally slides the tips of your fingers into his mouth and gently sucks on them. Once he feels he's kissed every part of your skin that's exposed, he reaches for the bottom of the top you've changed into and pulls it up, indicating he wants to take it off.

Completely in the mood now and wanting more, and forgetting that you're in forbidden territory, you help him by lifting your upper body up off the table slightly to allow him to pull the top all the way up. You lift your arms above your head to allow him to lift it off you. He's delighted to see more of the body that just minutes before had been on stage titillating a room full of people.

He proceeds to softly kiss the newly revealed velvety-soft skin around your bra, then down your sides, across your abdomen and down towards your nave. He reaches the top of the jeans you've changed into and lingers here, kissing along the line of skin on show just above them, back and forth.

After a while, he can't resist any more and he unbuttons and unzips your jeans. This allows him access to another small slither of skin above the thong you've changed into, which he proceeds to also kiss every part of.

Opening your jeans also unleashes the scent of your vagina somewhat. It's giving off a fragrance that drives him wild. He wants more of it and roughly pulls down your jeans hoping to inhale more. His face moves over your thong. You feel his nose touch it ever so faintly as he passes by. He inhales deeply as he does so to take in as much of your fragrance as he can.

He then starts kissing your legs. Once again, he takes care to softly kiss every last bit of them, first on the way down to your feet, where he concurrently pulls off your shoes and jeans, and then on the way back up towards your sexy thong. He even kisses your feet and toes as he wants both to taste and stimulate every bit of your body, desperate to make the time he has with you as incredible as possible for both of you.

On his way back up, he lingers a little on the area underneath your knees and at the top of your inside leg. He eventually reaches your thong, which is now visibly soaked through. He loves seeing this and once again deliberately brushes his nose against it as he kisses your inner leg so as to both tease you a little and get another breath of your vaginal fragrance.

He kisses all along the sides of your thong. He then lifts up each side of your thong in turn and kisses the area underneath. He catches a glimpse of your immaculately manicured pussy for the first time, and he's even more turned on by this – so much so he decides he needs to take your thong off, however much he loves the look and feel of it.

He pulls the sexy wet thong down your legs and off over your feet before replacing his face millimetres from your pussy. For him, your pussy looks glorious, and seeing the light glisten on the moisture that is seeping out of your vagina only makes it look ten times better. "Your pussy is beautiful – it looks so good," he whispers, looking up into your eyes for a change as he does so. "I want to eat it so much," he continues.

"Do it," you whisper back, breathlessly, overcome with excitement by his words and the prospect of being eaten out.

He removes his shirt and at the same time takes another deep breath to fully inhale the fragrance emanating from your freshly revealed vagina. He then re-applies his lips to your body, first again softly kissing your inner legs and thighs, then gently kissing every part of your pussy, back and forth, then moving down to kiss the opening to your vagina, where he ingests a mouthful of your juices.

He once again kisses all of your pussy, working from the bottom up to the top. It feels like he must be about to kiss your clitoris but he halts just before he reaches it and instead repeats the kissing of your labia and vaginal entrance, teasing you just as you've shortly beforehand teased him and a room full of other people.

He reaches the top of your pussy again but then again halts just before reaching your clitoris and then moves back down to your vagina, frustrating you once again with this teasing. Then he slowly works his way back up your pussy with his lips once again.

This time he continues upwards and makes contact with your clitoris. It feels sublime. You let out a gasp as he does so. He gently kisses it again. And again. And again. Then he moves away from it and starts kissing the rest of your pussy once again. You're frustrated by this but also loving being teased in this way and having the rest of your pussy stimulated as well. He continues kissing the rest of your pussy.

Eventually, he returns to your clitoris and you let out another gasp. He softly kisses it again. And again. And again. He then pauses, looks up into your eyes and says "Your pussy tastes so good." You then feel his tongue for the first time. He starts by slowly sliding it all the way from your perineum up over your vaginal entrance and over your pussy all the way to the edge of your clit. Once again, he pauses just before he reaches it. He moves back down and then again slowly slides his tongue from your perineum up over your vaginal entrance and labia to the edge of your clitoris. Once again, he pauses before he reaches it.

It drives you crazy with frustration. He moves back down to your perineum and then slowly glides his tongue once again from here all the way up to the edge of your clitoris. But this time there's only a momentary pause before his tongue collides with your clitoris. You let out another gasp as they meet and what you've been hoping for so long now finally comes to fruition.

Initially, he just leaves his tongue here, letting your clitoris adjust to having the warm moisture pressed against it. Then he starts gently sliding it back, forth and around, as if playing with it. You start moaning with pleasure as he does so.

He continues stimulating your clit with his tongue. You haven't had stimulation like this for so long and it feels incredible. You don't notice but seeing and hearing you writhe with pleasure turns him on even more too and his cock is throbbing inside his trousers.

He continues gliding his tongue over your clit but now sporadically mixes in movement of it over the rest of your pussy. Occasionally, he even inserts the tip of his tongue into your vagina and ingests further mouthfuls of your juices. The stimulation of all of your pussy, but particularly your clitoris, with his tongue feels divine. Your moaning gets louder and he can see your body writhe around more and more with pleasure.

He continues eating you out, loving every minute of seeing, hearing and feeling the impact he's having on you. The moaning and writhing continues. But after a while there's been no increase in volume or intensity of either and he realises that, however much you're enjoying this, it's not going to give you the orgasm he so desperately wants you to have. So, seemingly out of nowhere, he inserts two fingers into your vagina as he continues to lick you out. You let out an extra moan and breathless "Oh yeah," as he does so.

He initially just thrusts his fingers in and out of you, but then curls the tips of them so that they touch the top of your vaginal wall. He then starts stroking this area with them, continuing to lick your pussy, especially your clit, as he does so. It feels even better like this. You continue to moan and writhe, louder and more vigorously now.

He continues the double stimulation like this, delighting in every moan and gyration of your body. But again, your moaning and writhing plateaus and it seems clear that the status quo isn't going to be sufficient to bring you to the orgasm he so desperately wants to give you. So again, seemingly out of nowhere, he acts – you feel a finger from his other hand up against the entrance to your rectum.

Initially, he just gently caresses it by sliding the fingertip around the circumference of your ass, partly to stimulate the nerve endings there and partly to spread some of the vaginal juices it's collected en route. Then you feel this finger enter your tight anus and start slowly thrusting in and out of it. Allied with the licking of your pussy and the stroking of your G-spot, this feels unbelievable.

Your moaning and writhing picks up a notch. It's clear this has helped. Excited by this, he picks up the intensity of all three a little, pressing his tongue up against your pussy more firmly, stroking your G-spot more quickly and thrusting in and out of your ass both more quickly and deeply. It's exactly what you want and need. Your moaning and writhing reach a crescendo.

"That's it, let go and cum for me, baby," he whispers without interrupting the triple stimulation, sensing that you're on the brink. Your body tenses and then you let out an almighty howl of pleasure as you climax.

"Yeah, that's it, baby," he whispers as you do so, delighted that he's achieved what he desired so much, and more turned on than you can ever know by feeling, seeing, smelling and hearing this angel in paradise before him.

Eventually, your orgasm subsides. Seeing, hearing and feeling this, he gently removes his fingers and tongue from you and moves up to lie on top of you so you can just feel his body on yours and some closeness for a while to exacerbate the enjoyment you experience of your post-orgasmic bliss. You scarcely even notice his throbbing erection pressing up against you in your haze.

After a few minutes, you start to come out of your trance. You open your eyes to see him just gazing at you, his topless body pressed on top of yours. You stare intently back into his eyes, keen to maintain the intimacy but also trying to figure out what's going through his mind. Feeling so close to him, you decide you want more.

To his surprise, you remove your bra and then start to peel off his trousers and boxer shorts, maintaining eye contact with him throughout. The sight of your breasts, and the feel of your entire naked body pressed up against his drives him further wild.

Keeping your eyes fixated on his, you reach your hands down to his still-throbbing penis. You give the shaft of it a quick stroke to size it up, feel just how hard it is and let him know that you're thinking about his pleasure too. You then move his rock-solid cock, now both comforted and further excited from the feel of your hand around it, until it's nestled up against your vaginal opening.

"I want you inside me," you whisper. Still looking into his eyes, you move your hands away from his cock and round on to his lower back. You gently pull him towards you. He enters you. You both let out a gasp as he does so. The feel of his throbbing erection penetrating you is exhilarating. The feel of your soaking wet pussy around his cock is incredible.

Still looking into each other's eyes, he starts slowly thrusting in and out of you. With him so hard and you so wet, every thrust glides smoothly. The intimacy between the two of you is intense, like there's electricity running between your bodies – his penis filling you to complete the circuit – as you feel him thrust into you and his body brush up against yours as he looks into your eyes. He continues thrusting, still slowly but now more deeply, into you, watching your reaction the whole time. You start to quietly gasp nearly every time he thrusts as you feel his cock reach your vaginal wall.

Matters continue like this for a long time. He's getting so much pleasure and being able to see and feel you enjoy it too he doesn't want to change a thing. But eventually he decides it's time that he tries something else to increase your pleasure. "Want to go for a ride?" he whispers.

"OK," you respond, not really wanting to move and unsure as to what he has in mind but nevertheless open to it.

He squeezes his arms between your back and the desk, pulls you up towards him, as he too lifts his upper body up, and then picks you fully up, backing away from the desk as he does so. You wrap your legs around him and he moves his arms up a little before similarly wrapping them around you. You continue looking into each other's eyes the whole time.

He begins thrusting in and out of you once again. It's not quite as deep from this angle but the intimacy is enhanced further by the way your bodies are entangled. For him, having your hot naked body wrapped around him so that so much of your soft velvety skin is touching his while he thrusts in and out of you feels phenomenal.

"You're incredible," he whispers. He then can't resist but to break the eye contact for once to kiss you on the lips so that even more of your bodies are touching, and as if to reinforce to you how much he values the intimacy between you.

Both acts and his choice of words catch you by surprise a little but you appreciate them and kiss him back when he places his lips on yours. He keeps you suspended in mid-air like this, your bodies entwined, for several minutes.

There's gasping and panting aplenty from both of you as he continues to thrust in and out of you with his rock-hard cock. The closeness and warmth of your bodies rubbing against each other causes you both to perspire a little, him more than you. Your gorgeous body begins to glisten in the light as a result.

But again, after a while, he decides that it's time to switch things up. He's conscious that, although he can tell you're enjoying it, there's more pleasure that could be had and he wants to give that to you. He carries you over to the sofa, lays you down, and recommences his thrusting into you briefly before he unexpectedly withdraws, much to the chagrin of both of you, and quietly says "Turn around."

Although a little reticent, thinking that he is now going to undermine all the intimacy that's gone before by just fucking you hard doggy style for his own gratification, you do as you're told, getting on all fours so that your pert ass faces him, and he can see all of the rear of your body in all its glory.

The assumption that gave rise to your reticence couldn't be more misplaced. Although he does re-enter you and begin thrusting deep inside you, doggy style, with his hands placed on your hips for leverage, there are only a few thrusts like this before he changes things again slightly, and these initial thrusts are only to facilitate the subsequent transition.

He pauses, takes his hands off your hips, leans his upper body down until his torso makes contact with your back and his face hangs just above the back of your head. "Lie down," he whispers, applying his weight onto you a little to encourage you to do as he says.

You duly oblige and as you lower yourself, he comes with you, his rock-solid cock still deep inside you. You lie flat on the sofa, he lies flat on top of you. You turn your head to one side to make it more comfortable for you lying like this but it's not enough to enable you to see him. He then grabs your hands, moves them high above your head and places his on top of them, holding yours down.

He begins to rock back and forth inside you once again, slowly at first. The position feels intense – not just because he's deep inside you and rubbing up against your G-spot but also because a) he's dominating you and you're essentially powerless to go anywhere with the weight of his naked body pressed on top of yours and b) you feel closeness from having his entire body nestled against yours. He continues thrusting in and out of you like this and, as he does so, moves his head from its position draped directly above yours over to the side yours is facing so you can see him.

Once you've locked eye contact for a few seconds so you know he's very much thinking of you, he starts kissing your neck and ears whilst thrusting in and out of you. He then starts interspersing this with whispering right in your ear. "You feel incredible," he begins. "I want you to feel as much pleasure as I am," he continues. "Do you like it like this?" he initially finishes with.

"Yes," you breathlessly whisper back as he continues to thrust into you and kiss your neck and ear.

"How about we try and make it even better?" he softly replies.

"Oh yeah," you respond, unsure of what he has in mind but happy to go along with it given how much you're enjoying things as they are and everything he's done so far.

You then feel him place your right hand against your left underneath his left, high above your head, and then bring his right arm down to your right side. He then wriggles it underneath you, somehow finding a gap between your abdomen and the sofa. He continues wriggling it further and further under you until you feel his hand reach your pussy. He leaves his hand here, takes two of his fingers and starts caressing your clitoris with them.

"Ohhh," you moan, as you feel the extra stimulation.

"Like that, baby?" he whispers in your ear.

"Yes," you breathlessly reply.

He continues thrusting into you, while pinning you down with his body and left hand, and stroking your clitoris with his right. The combination of domination, closeness and having both your vagina and clitoris simultaneously stimulated feels incredible.

He supplements this by continuing to intersperse kissing you with occasional whispers in your ear to juxtapose the domination and increased physical stimulation with intimacy and stimulation of your mind. This, allied with the feeling of his breath on you, the vibration on the back of your neck when he speaks, and the smell of his aftershave is a sensory overload.

Your whole body (as well as your mind), is being stimulated to a greater or lesser extent as even his legs and feet are on top of yours and gently rubbing against them as he continues to thrust inside you. Going out of your mind from the all-encompassing stimulation, you start moaning repeatedly, louder and louder, and your body starts writhing around once again underneath his.

"Oh yeah," he whispers in your ear, feeling and hearing this. It's clear his change of plan is working, and hearing and feeling you in ecstasy like this, both from inside and out, serves to turn him on even more than he already is.

You feel his cock throb even more inside you. You can tell from this he may now be on the brink of climax, which turns you on even more, causing you to moan even louder, and writhe around even more vigorously.

This in turn turns him on even more. He can't even talk now, he's so aroused and getting so much pleasure from you; his whispering in your ear turns to groaning, louder and louder. He speeds up the pace and intensity of his thrusting into you and the caressing of your clitoris, both because he can hear and feel this is what you want and because his own arousal necessitates it.

You're now so close to orgasm yourself. "Yes, yes, yes," you scream as he continues to thrust into you, now really deep, fast and hard, stroke your clitoris, groan repeatedly in your ear and keep you pinned down despite your now-frenetic writhing around.

Hearing this screaming and feeling you at the point of climax, he can't control himself any longer. He lets out a roar right into your ear as his eyes roll back into his head, his body goes into frenzy and he explodes inside you. Hearing and feeling this sends you over the edge. You join him in climactic heaven and scream out his name before falling silent in the midst of your ecstasy.

The Balcony

It's a Saturday night. You're out at a bar with one of your long-time girlfriends. You have no particular agenda other than to relax, spend some quality time with her and generally have a good night. You've made an effort to look ravishing nonetheless – make-up, perfume, high heels and a low-cut blue dress (but little else), on.

The bar is about three-quarters full – there's a constant hum of chatting and laughing amongst the dance music playing in the background and it's busy but not repressively so. You and your friend have a small table to yourselves. All the other tables are taken and quite a few patrons are stood in between them.

The bar is dark but with strategically placed sexy lighting. The bar itself is long and straight with two shelves at the back that are covered end-to-end in bottles of every kind of spirit you can think of, and there's a mirror behind it enabling everyone at the bar to clandestinely check both themselves and everyone else out when they're ordering drinks.

You and your friend have been here for about an hour. You're just finishing your second cocktail. Everything's going well. You're enjoying catching up with her, getting to laugh every now and then and generally enjoy the vibe.

You both finish your cocktails. It's your round so you leave your friend at the table and head to the bar. There are a number of people there and you have to wait a few minutes to order. As you do so, a group of four guys that have evidently just arrived walk up to the bar right behind you to join the throng trying to buy a drink.

You can't help but notice their presence behind you and you subtly check them out using the mirror on the wall behind the bar while the bartender whips up your cocktails. Your heart skips a beat as you discover that all four of them are incredibly attractive.

You turn back to process what you've just seen. After a few seconds, one of the guys, 'Guy A', realises the queue for drinks isn't really moving. He looks around, sees you waiting in front and decides to lean towards you and ask "How long have you been waiting?"

Although initially being a little unsettled by having such attractive men so close to you, the few seconds since laying eyes on them has allowed you to regain your composure. You look the guy in the eye with a naughty expression and say in the sexiest possible way "For what?"

He clocks the flirtation and lets a smile spread slightly across his face before responding calmly and in an equally flirtatious manner with "You tell me."

The other three guys, 'Guy B', 'Guy C' and 'Guy D', are watching you and listening. At that point the discourse between you is broken by the barman who places your completed cocktails on the bar next to you. You tap your card to pay, pick up the drinks and turn to return to your table.

All four guys are still looking at you, particularly the one you exchanged words with. Seeing this, you pause momentarily to contemplate the situation. Drinks in hand, you make a split-second decision that there might be some fun for the taking so you say "Want to join us?" as you look at all the guys in turn, starting with Guy A, while gesturing with your head to the table where your friend is sitting.

With that, you strut back to your table and set down the drinks. A few minutes of talking with your friend and sipping on your cocktails pass while the guys remain at the bar trying to buy drinks of their own. Every now and then your eyes wonder back to them and sometimes your eyes meet with one of them when you notice they're looking back at you. Eventually, the guys are served and they proceed to walk over to your table with their drinks, as invited.

"Hi," says Guy A, firstly looking at you and then your friend. He introduces himself and then the other three guys in turn. You reciprocate. Whilst you and your friend sit on your stools, the other guys stand, perched against the table, two either side.

"How's your night going?" Guy A says to try and open up the conversation.

"It's going great – now," your friend replies with a childlike smirk.

"I really like this place," you chime in. "The drinks are great – and the clientele of course." A cheeky smile sneaks across your face as you say this while looking at the guys. You then suckle on the straw in your cocktail in a deliberately provocative manner while you have their gaze.

"That's quite a technique you've got there," Guy B says, attempting a little innuendo of his own.

"Oh, that's nothing," you retort, again with a cheeky smile and seductive eyes.

The discourse between the six of you continues like this – vague attempts to try and open up the conversation tempered by flirty, innuendo-fuelled responses – for another twenty minutes or so. At this point, Guy D notices everyone's drinks are either empty or close thereto so he asks "So what are you ladies up to for the rest of the night?"

Now feeling comfortable and confident that there's fun to be had with these guys, for once you don't give a provocative response and simply say "We don't have anything specific planned."

Encouraged by this, Guy D says "Well, I have an apartment just around the corner so we could all go back there and carry on if you fancy it?"

Your eyes turn from Guy D to your friend. You look at her quizzically, as if to say "How about it?"

She very quickly and subtly raises her eyebrows as if to say "Oh yes!"

You turn back to Guy D and say "Sure." With that, those that haven't quite finished their drinks do so and set their glasses down, and the six of you walk out of the bar single file.

It's dark outside but with light emanating from the moon and the streetlights, bars, restaurants and residential towers of the surrounding locale. It's comparatively quiet outside – there's no traffic in the area and the only noise of note is the muffled music and murmuring of the people in the surrounding bars and restaurants.

When you're all outside, Guy D turns to you and your friend and says "It's just around the corner," pointing to a T-junction at the end of the road about forty metres away. Guy D leads the way and the group all walk to the T-junction and then turn right.

"We're heading up there," Guy D says, pointing up ahead to a large modern-looking tower block about 50 metres ahead. Again, Guy D leads the way and the rest of the group follows.

The six of you arrive in the reception of the apartment block. Guy D continues walking towards the lift and presses the call button. The lift arrives and all six of you enter, the guys strategically taking up places in the four corners, and you and your friend in the middle.

It's not a big lift and there's barely a space between you all. Guy D presses the button for floor thirty-seven. You spot that there are buttons for only forty floors and start pondering whether this means Guy D's pad is rather special.

As the lift starts to ascend, the sexual tension is palpable. You feel as though testosterone is engulfing you, penetrating your every pore. No-one says a word, a sense of anticipation in the air precluding thoughts of ordinary conversation, but in such a small, enclosed space you can't help but inhale each other's scents and breath, and, despite occasional efforts to avoid eye contact, your eyes can't help but look at the guys and sporadically meet with theirs.

The lift arrives at floor thirty-seven and the doors open. Guy D gets out first and leads the way along the corridor to his apartment door. Once again, the rest of the group follow. En route you notice that, aside from one other door at the opposite end of the corridor, there's no other door on this floor. It therefore hits you that Guy D's apartment must be huge, given the scale of the building that you'd seen from outside.

Guy D unlocks the door, walks in and turns on the lights. You all follow. Your attention is momentarily taken away from the guys because the apartment is stunning: Large, open-plan, beautifully lit with dimmable spotlights, soft furnishings, a large three-piece sofa that you quickly estimate could hold up to ten people, a fish tank, its own bar area and large floor-to-ceiling windows that open out onto a large balcony overlooking the rest of the city and the river below.

"This is quite a place you've got here," you say, understatedly.

"Thanks. Come in and make yourselves at home," he replies plainly while opening the balcony door and gesturing towards the balcony beyond.

It's a very warm and still night and you're happy to oblige. As you walk through the open plan living/kitchen/dining area, you notice a huge bedroom through a door on the left out of the corner of your eye. Guy D presses a button on a remote control to set some chill-out music playing and then walks over to the bar area while the other five of you take a seat on the large luxuriant outdoor sofa outside.

The vista from the balcony is breath-taking – the river reflecting the moonlight down below, flanked by high-rise buildings on either side as far as the eye can see – and you try and take it in as you sit down. "Quite a view," Guy C says, looking at you with a smile that indicates more than a hint of double-entendre.

Recognising that the scenery surrounding you isn't all he was referring to. "Yes, it is," you reply, looking back at him and returning his smile.

"Do you come up here often?" you continue.

"Only on special occasions," Guy C replies, again looking at you with a smile.

At this point, Guy D comes out onto the balcony clutching a cocktail in each hand. He passes one to you and one to your friend. "My take on a 'Sex On The Beach' – let's call it 'Sex On The Balcony!'" he proclaims.

"Mmm, let's enjoy some 'Sex On The Balcony'," you say, as you turn to your friend, raise your eyebrows at her with a faint smile, and take a sip.

You and your friend are impressed. The cocktail is strong but not overpowering; there's a hint of acidity but it's offset by enough sweetness. It's poured over crushed ice with rosemary and a cherry for decoration. It's borderline bar-standard.

"This is definitely the best 'Sex On The Balcony' I've ever had," you remark, wryly.

"Maybe we should all have some 'Sex On The Balcony' then," Guy D replies after a very brief pause, his eyes flitting between you and your friend as he does so, now with a more serious expression on his face. There's ambiguity as to whether this is a statement or a question, but you treat it as the latter.

You're very aroused by now and you can tell your friend is too. You pause, looking first at Guy D and then at Guy A, Guy B and Guy C as you contemplate, before replying "I definitely think you should all have 'Sex On The Balcony' with us."

"What do you think?" Guy D says, turning to your friend.

"I agree – let's all have 'Sex On The Balcony'," she replies, the desire evident in her voice and eyes.

"Well, you can have as much 'Sex On The Balcony' tonight as you want," Guy D says, lowering his voice.

With that, he slowly moves closer to you both. He calmly takes each of your drinks from your hands and puts them down on the table, before edging right up to you until his body is a matter of millimetres from yours, staring into your eyes as he does so. He gently puts his hands on your hips, then tilts his head to one side, whispers, "I want to give you the night of your life," in your ear and starts softly kissing your neck.

You feel a tingle rip through your body as he does so, as if he's plugged your neck into an electrical current. As Guy D continues softly kissing your neck, Guy A, Guy B and Guy C stand and watch, seemingly waiting to see your reaction.

After about thirty seconds, it's clear that you want this and you're thoroughly enjoying it. Seeing this, Guy A slowly moves up behind you. You feel him brush up against you and then put his hands just below where Guy D's are.

"Can I join in?" he whispers in your ear.

"Yes," you quietly mutter back, somewhat distracted by the electricity running through you courtesy of Guy D.

You then feel Guy A start softly kissing the other side of your neck. The feel of two very attractive guys up against you, one each side, with their hands and lips on you in different places feels thrilling.

You closed your eyes when Guy D started kissing you so at this stage you have no idea that, while Guy A approached you, Guy B and Guy C slowly walked towards your friend and replicated with her what Guy A and Guy D are doing to you, even though they're only about a metre away from you. She's enjoying the experience just as much as you are.

You feel Guy D and Guy A start moving their hands over your body, gently fondling your side, your arms, your ass and your breasts. "Your skin is so velvety soft," Guy D whispers as he starts moving his kissing down from your neck towards the top of your low-cut dress. Guy A does likewise down your back. You feel tingles everywhere from the stimulation of the different parts of your body.

When Guy A reaches the top of your dress with his lips, he starts to peel its zip down your back, revealing more of your skin. His lips continue working their way down your back and his hands revert to stroking different parts of your body. With the zip undone, your dress falls down below your breasts at the front, inviting Guy D to continue moving his lips down onto your breasts.

With their bodies so close to you, you also notice for the first time their erections pressed up against you. Guy D and Guy A continue kissing your breasts and back, and you feel their hands stroking you virtually everywhere except your lower legs and between your thighs. Though they're not touching your pussy, the stimulation of other areas is making you very wet down there.

As if they can taste or smell that, Guy A starts to remove your dress fully. With more flesh revealed, Guy D and Guy A start to kiss and stroke the areas of your skin they haven't been able to until now – your abdomen, your lower back, the top of your legs and beyond. It's bliss.

You've still got your eyes closed and you don't even contemplate opening them as if it's a dream that you don't want to wake up from. With you now wearing nothing but your thong (and shoes), and having had the combination of Guy D and Guy A kissing and stroking you everywhere except your groin (and feet), Guy D decides it's time to find out where you're at and ever so slowly slides his hand up your inner leg until it touches your thong. You tense as you feel your pussy touched by one of them for the first time, through your underwear. Your pussy's been craving that touch now for quite some time.

"Does that feel good?" Guy D whispers.

"Yes," you half-whisper, half-moan back.

As he touches you, Guy D can feel that your thong is soaked. He lets his hand linger for a little while, very slowly moving it around to stroke different parts of your pussy through your thong. But now in the knowledge that you're so wet, he decides it's time to step things up somewhat. He moves his hand away from your thong and, a little out of the blue, puts his hands back on your hips, lifts you up, carries you over to the outdoor sofa and lays you down on it, removing his shirt, trousers and boxer shorts, lowering himself on top of you as he does so.

"You look so good," he whispers, looking into your eyes. You feel his body on top of you and his erection pressing up against your pussy through your thong. It feels exhilarating.

The shock of being lifted up prompted you to open your eyes and doing so alerted you to the fact that your

77

friend is already laid out naked on another part of the sofa, being licked out by Guy C while she sucks Guy B's cock. The sight of this arouses you even more.

Guy A notices you noticing the other three engaging in their oral antics and concludes from the way your eyes light up that you want something similar. As Guy D pulls down your thong to reveal your soaking wet pussy, Guy A undresses himself.

You just lie there on your back, numb with anticipation, watching the show of one guy removing your thong and shoes to leave you completely naked and the other undressing himself to reveal his hot body, the sight of which adds to your excitement. They're looking at you as you watch them. With you laid out in all your glory, you see two sets of eyes and two big, hard dicks staring back at you.

"Your pussy looks so good. I want to eat it," Guy D says, still staring into your eyes.

"Do it," you reply, opening your legs.

Guy D shuffles down between your open legs. He starts slowly, softly kissing the top of your thighs and then all around your pussy – but not the pussy itself so as to tease you. Eventually, his lips descend upon your pussy. You let out a slight moan as his lips make contact with it for the first time.

He kisses all of it, initially so softly he's barely touching it. He pauses briefly to whisper, "You taste so good," before pressing his lips more firmly onto your pussy, firstly kissing the opening of your vagina and then slowly upwards towards your clitoris.

He doesn't quite reach your clit and instead reverses back down towards your vagina. You're both frustrated and delighted by the teasing in equal measure. When he reaches your vagina, he takes out his tongue and slides it around the opening, imbibing a mouthful of your juices as he does so. You let out another moan as he does so.

He continues to slide his tongue around the opening of your vagina for a few seconds before slowly working it up towards your clitoris. This time he makes contact and it feels incredible. You let out another moan, louder this time.

Guy D stays focused on your clit, delicately sliding his tongue over and around it. As you start to get used to the wonderful feeling, you realise that Guy A is still there watching, his big erection still pointed right at you.

"Come here," you say, looking back at him. "I want you in my mouth."

He moves towards you and stops by the sofa, close enough that he can dangle his cock right above your face. You take it in your hand and start stroking the shaft, before opening your mouth and placing the end of it inside you, looking into his eyes as you do so. You start gently sucking on it. Guy A lets out a slight moan as you do so. "That feels so good," he whispers, as you continue sucking him.

As you continue fellating him, you see out of the corner of your eye that your friend is now stood up and bent over, about a metre behind Guy D, elbows on the wall of the balcony, lower arms dangled over the edge with the city below. She's being pummelled from behind by Guy B, with Guy C knelt down in front of her, licking her clit. Your friend is in ecstasy, repeatedly moaning, louder and louder. The sight and sound of this adds to your arousal.

You try to sustain your focus on Guy D and Guy A. The pleasure of Guy D licking your pussy means you're struggling to fully focus on Guy A and every few seconds you stop momentarily to let out a moan right into Guy A's cock.

The three of you continue like this for quite some time. Guy D continues to expertly perform cunnilingus on you. Every now and again his tongue deviates from your clit to other parts of your pussy – sometimes the outside of your pussy lips, sometimes the inside of them, sometimes down and around your vagina and sometimes actually inserting his tongue into your vagina to ingest another mouthful of your juices.

He continues devouring you, seemingly content to eat you out all night. His warm, moist tongue feels incredible and the way he plays with your clit with it is driving you wild. Every so often he varies the speed and pressure. And just to add to the experience, every so often he pauses ever so briefly to murmur some naughty words to you, "You like having my tongue in your cunt?" after one of his dalliances into your vagina. "You taste so good. Your pussy smells so good. Your pussy lips are so supple." You can't get enough of the oral stimulation.

Eventually, you decide that you need something more and that Guy D deserves some attention. You remove Guy A from your mouth but keep hold of his shaft with your right hand, as if scared it may never come back if you let go. You gently push Guy D's face away from your pussy with your left hand, reach for his right hand, which he gives you, and then pull him towards you until you can feel his body right up against you, and his erection right up against your pussy. You stop pulling him towards you at this point. You're staring into each other's eyes. You're trying to tell him with your eyes that you want him to enter you. He thinks that's what you're saying but wants to be sure. "Can I penetrate you?" he whispers.

You don't say a word and instead simply nod your head, still staring into his eyes. Very slowly, you feel his hard cock slide into you. It's big and it fills you. It feels divine. You're still looking into each other's eyes as he starts thrusting in and out of you. But you're careful to make sure Guy A is suitably attended to as well so, while being ridden by Guy D, you place Guy A back in your mouth and start sucking him again. This time, you keep your eyes on Guy D as do this, though, as if to say "Look how much I love having cock in me" to him. As if reading this message, he starts thrusting harder and faster, as if to reply "Maybe you do but I want to make you love having my cock in you the best".

The harder thrusting feels so good and you let out a big moan, which for Guy A manifests itself as vibrating to complement your sucking. He enjoys it and you feel his cock harden further in your mouth. Guy D takes your moan as validation to continue like this and he starts to really give it to you. You can feel him so deep inside your pussy and it feels wonderful.

You start moaning regularly from the pleasure, which in turn acts like a vibrator for Guy A, who starts to moan himself from the pleasure. Guy D's absolutely loving being able to fuck you like this. He's so aroused by your hot naked body, your intoxicating scent, the touch of your skin against his, the feel of your soaking wet pussy engulfing his hard cock.

He doesn't want to stop but, to your surprise, suddenly he does. He's decided he wants to try something else. He lifts his upper body up, slides his hands underneath your lower back and proceeds to pick you up, firstly so you're astride him with your legs wrapped around him while he's on his knees on the sofa where he starts thrusting into you again for a few seconds, and then latterly so he's standing and you're suspended in mid-air completely wrapped around him.

The sudden change in position meant you had to let Guy A's cock go en route and instead dangle your arms around Guy D. Guy A stands waiting, watching as Guy D starts fucking you once more. It feels great, not just from the penetration but also from the masculinity of having him holding you up at the same time, his toned body brushed up against yours and your arms around him, holding him close to you.

Guy D continues fucking you like this, increasingly furiously. His gamble on change of position has paid off: He's absolutely loving it here and can see and hear from you that you're getting serious pleasure too.

Unbeknownst to you, he then beckons to Guy A to come closer. Guy A obliges, and you can feel his presence behind you while you're being pummelled by Guy D. Guy A's skin brushes up against your back once again. "You have such a great ass. I'd love to fuck it. Would you like me to do that?" he whispers in your ear.

You're so lost in the carnage with Guy D you can barely respond, but you manage to muster a, "Yeahhh!" – a combination between consent to Guy A and a scream of pleasure.

Next thing you know, you can feel Guy A's rock-hard penis, still well-lubricated from your saliva, entering your ass and begin to thrust into you as well. "Oh yeah," you shout as Guy A and Guy D simultaneously fuck you. The feeling of having both your holes filled and fucked is out of this world.

Every now and then you here Guy D and Guy A mutter some words at you: "Ah yeah!"; "How do you like this?"; Your tight ass feels so good!"; "Your wet pussy feels amazing."

In the midst of this, behind Guy D you can see your friend now being fucked by both Guy B and Guy C. Guy B is laid on the sofa behind Guy A's head, with your friend lying on top of him with her back to him, and Guy C on top of her facing her. Guy C is in her pussy and Guy B is in her ass. They're both screwing her hard and fast.

She's in heaven and her moaning has long since turned to screams. The screams reach a crescendo to let you know that the double-teaming from Guy B and Guy C has brought her to orgasm. You get turned on even more by seeing their threesome going on and hearing her howling.

Witnessing her orgasm brings to your attention how close you now are to your own. The combination of being double-teamed in mid-air by these hot guys, their hands all over your body, their skin up against yours, their own moans (and words) letting you know how much pleasure you're giving them – all al fresco against the backdrop of a stunning moonlit city scene – is all-consuming and blowing your mind.

But before you know it, you're now encircled by Guy B, Guy C and your friend as well. Her orgasm behind her, the three of them turn their attention to you.

"Can we join in?" Guy B murmurs.

You can barely utter a response. At the third attempt, you manage some sort of noise resembling a "Yes" and an accompanying nod amongst the body shaking caused by the double penetration.

With Guy D at (and in) your front and Guy A at (and in) your rear, Guy B and Guy C move up next to you on either side and start grabbing your breasts and stroking your legs. Your friend, meanwhile, moves up behind Guy D, presses her body up against his and then reaches her arms round either side until they reach Guy B and Guy C's dicks, which are still perfectly erect. She starts simultaneously kissing Guy D's back and tossing Guy B and Guy C off, their hard dicks and her hands sporadically brushing against your sides in the process.

You, a screaming goddess in the middle, are now surrounded by four incredibly attractive, seriously aroused men, all moaning with the pleasure you and your friend are giving them. All four guys have their eyes fixed firmly on you, two of them deep inside of you, two of them having their dicks fondled up against your sides.

Guy D and Guy A continue to furiously thrust into you, with Guy A now sporadically interchanging kissing and lightly biting your neck at the same time. Guy B and Guy C continue to each fondle one of your breasts but then each move one of their hands away from stroking other parts of your body towards your pussy. There's barely space for their hands between Guy D's body and yours but they manage to squeeze them in and you feel them start stroking your clit from either side.

"Ohhhh," you scream as they start to do so. This is the final straw. The stimulating of all parts of your body – internally and externally – and all of your senses, now with the addition of the icing on the clitoral cake, sends you over the edge. Your body goes into complete spasm and you let out a shriek that seems to last an eternity as the ecstasy consumes you. You lose your mind. It's as though you've gone to another place.

You're so lost in your own orgasm that you barely notice that this raging goddess at the centre of it all has led the throbbing cocks of Guy D and Guy A to explode their seminal fluid into both of your holes and Guy B and Guy C to ejaculate all over each of your sides – expertly guided by the hands of your friend so as to land on different parts of your skin.

Initially, it's only their long accompanying grunts and groans that bring to your attention that they're also all climaxing inside, all over and because of you. But then you feel their warm spunk flooding into your pussy and ass, and spurting all over your sides. It feels dirty but thrilling. You love it and it just adds to the intensity of your own orgasm, which seems to just go on and on.

You don't want it to ever end but eventually it starts to subside, which coincides with a slowing of the thrusting inside of you from both ends as Guy D and Guy A's own orgasms come to an end.

Very slowly, the six of you untangle your naked bodies: Your friend lets go of Guy B and Guy C's softening penises and they shuffle back away from you. Your friend shuffles back away from Guy D. Guy A withdraws from your ass. This feels especially disappointing as you've absolutely loved having him there and his body pressed up behind you. Then, finally, Guy D lifts you up and off his cock before lowering you back to the ground. It's a metaphor for your own return to earth from the heaven you've just been in.

You stand there, feeling a bit feint and somewhat overwhelmed. You look around and the other five are all looking at you, smiling. You have no idea but you're a complete mess – your hair and make-up has gone all over the place, your skin is glistening with perspiration, there are red marks on various parts of your body from the rubbing of bodies up against it and the biting of your neck, and there's semen everywhere, sliding down your sides and dripping out of your vagina and ass.

Somewhat counterintuitively, it's seriously hot – these are all just symptoms of how naughty you've been – and the guys are all loving the view, perhaps trying to firmly plant the image in their memory so that they can reuse it to keep them entertained when they're alone one night in future.

Eventually, you feel some of the spunk dripping out of you and decide you should clean yourself up. You avert your eyes from the others as a result. But Guy D doesn't want you to clean up (and nor do Guy A, Guy B and Guy C), so, before you get a chance to go anywhere or say anything, he breaks the sort of silent stand-off by walking over to the table, picking up the two cocktails, and walking over to you and your friend with them. Holding them out to offer them to you both, he says *"Want some Sex On The Balcony?"*

Liquor in the front, poker in the rear

It's a Thursday evening. You've arranged to meet one of your girl friends at a cocktail bar for a long overdue catch-up. You make it to the bar at the agreed time. When you arrive, there's no sign of your friend so you just take a seat at one of the empty tables.

Before you've even really settled, a waiter comes over and asks if you'd like a drink. You haven't even had a chance to look at the menu waiting on the table so you ask him, "What's your best cocktail?"

"A lot of people like our cherry daiquiri," he replies, opening the menu and pointing to it.

"That sounds great, I'll have one of those," you say with a smile.

The waiter walks off and you sit back, relax and, while you wait for your friend, look around to admire the décor of the bar – one you haven't been to before. You're surprised that a bar as beautiful as this is so quiet for a Thursday evening but one positive of this is the quick service – the waiter returns with your cocktail in no more than two minutes. You take a sip and it tastes great.

You're now feeling really good; you've had a reasonable day at work and have nothing hanging over you so you've already forgotten about the office, and you're excited to see your friend and to enjoy some lovely drinks while hearing all about her adventures since you last saw her.

After about five minutes of enjoying being able to relax with a delicious cocktail, you decide to check your phone to see if your friend has messaged to say she's running a bit late. There's no message but you don't think anything of it and continue to enjoy the moment.

Another five minutes passes and you check your phone again as your friend is usually someone to reliably arrive on time or message if there's been any delay. Still nothing.

After another five minutes you start to feel both slightly worried and slightly annoyed. You're already halfway through your cocktail and the enjoyment of the relaxing solitude has started to turn to boredom.

Then a notification appears on your phone – it's your friend: "I'm so sorry, my boyfriend's mother's been taken to hospital and I've had to go with him so I'm not going to be able to make it."

You feel both annoyed (as you'd been really looking forward to the evening and held off plans with other people specifically) and sympathetic in equal measure. You send a sympathetic reply and then prepare yourself to leave and go home.

You speed up your sipping and soon finish your cocktail. You get the waiter's attention and ask for the bill. He soon arrives with it and you settle up. You stand up to leave. But as you do so a man wanders over, almost as if from nowhere, and says to you, "You're not leaving, are you?"

"Well, I was about to," you reply.

"Can you not stay for another drink?" he enquires.

You pause to contemplate. You'd half-noticed him while he was sat alone at the bar – one of the few other people there – but not really paid any attention as your mind was on other things. Now in full focus, you notice that he's gorgeous, well-presented in a perfectly-fitted suit and shirt, and with a glint in his eyes that makes you believe there's adventure to be had. As you'd cleared your calendar anyway and therefore now have no plans after your friend's sudden withdrawal, you decide you've got nothing to lose by staying for a drink and seeing what happens.

"OK," you say, and promptly sit back down.

He sits down at the seat opposite to you. "You're on cherry daiquiri, right?" he says.

"Yes," you answer, a slight smile emerging across your face as you do so as you're somewhat impressed that he's paid that much attention before you've even met.

The guy hails the waiter and orders for you both: "Peroni for me and cherry daiquiri for this beautiful young lady," he says, looking in your direction as he does so.

As the waiter walks away, the guy begins to converse in earnest: "So what brings you here tonight?"

You explain how you've been left in the lurch by your friend.

"That's a pity, you must be really disappointed," he responds. "But maybe the situation with your friend happened for a reason and tonight's going to be your lucky night."

"Oh, is that right?" you reply.

There's a slight pause and then he asks, "Do you like poker?"

"I love poker!" you respond.

"Would you like to play tonight?" he enquires.

You again pause to contemplate momentarily but, concluding once again that you're free for the evening and have nothing to lose, and that your limited interaction with this guy so far has been so good that you're excited about what more could come of the evening if you stay with him, you ultimately answer, "Sure."

"Great," he says, a smile this time emerging across his face.

The waiter arrives with your drinks. "Cheers," he says as he raises his glass towards you, looking you squarely in the eyes.

"Cheers," you reply with a smile, likewise raising your glass.

As you slowly consume your drinks, the guy asks about you – when you last played poker, what else you're in to and other similar questions that show interest without being too probing. You answer honestly and openly, the conversation flows well and you find yourself laughing from time to time.

As you get towards the end of your drink, he says, "Ready for some poker?"

"OK," you reply.

The guy pays and then turns to you and says, "Follow me."

He leads you out of the bar and down the street. After only about 50 metres, he says, "Here we are."

He unlocks the front door to an innocuous-looking building – what appears to be an ordinary four-storey residential terrace. You enter the front door and see a corridor leading to other doors and a staircase leading down to another door. It's all rather dark, with only limited dim old-fashioned lighting to aid your visibility.

He leads you down the stairs. As you reach the door at the bottom, you see a sign above it that reads 'Liquor in the front, poker in the rear.' You're not sure whether to be amused or concerned by what you read but, as he opens the door, you put it out of your mind and follow him in.

You're a little taken aback by what greets you – a dimly-lit room with nothing in it aside from a large poker table in pristine condition in the centre, spot-lit by a large lamp hanging from the ceiling above it, a few old paintings depicting poker games hung on the walls and a bland wooden door at the back of the room. There are six stunning old-fashioned leather seats surrounding the table and six equal stacks of poker chips sat on the table, one by each seat. In the background, 1920s-style piano music is gently playing.

Four of the seats are taken by what you immediately notice are four extremely handsome men, each as well-dressed and groomed as the stranger that you accompanied from the bar. The conversation that they had been engaged in comes to an abrupt halt as you enter. There's a silence as they stare at you and you take in the scene you're presented with.

Eventually, one of the men at the table breaks the silence: "Hi, are you joining us for a game?" he says, with a faint but friendly smile.

"Yes," you reply, likewise emitting a faint smile and turning to look at the man you met at the bar as you do so, as if to request confirmation from him – or at least his help with the awkward discourse.

"This beautiful young lady I just met says she loves a game of poker so I invited her to join us," the guy from the bar says.

"Take a seat and make yourself comfortable," the guy from the bar says to you. "Can I get you a drink? We don't have the ingredients for a cherry daiquiri but I'm sure we can find something else to satiate you," he continues as you sit down to join the others.

"Sure, I'm easy so why don't you surprise me?" you reply.

With that, the man from the bar disappears through the inauspicious door at the back of the room. There's then another awkward pause as the five of you are sat at the table, four handsome guys silently transfixed on you and you in return surveying them one by one, unsure whether or not to speak.

The awkwardness is broken when the guy from the bar returns through the door. He sets your drink down in the dedicated drinks holder on the table in front of you, and then sits down at the vacant seat next to you with a drink of his own.

"Cheers," he says, raising his glass towards you.

"Cheers," the other men follow, with the drinks they already have.

You all clink glasses and then take a sip. You can't put your finger on what's in your drink but it tastes good – sweet yet potent but not overly so.

"So, aside from the fact that we play no limit Texas hold'em with which you're familiar, we do things a bit differently at this club," the guy from the bar says. "We have a high stakes game and a very high stakes game. Or of course if neither takes your fancy then you don't have to take part, although that would be a shame. As it's your first time here we'll let you decide which you want to play. The high stakes game has a £10,000 buy-in – winner takes all."

He then falls silent, as if to leave you to process his words. After a few seconds you ask, "What's the very high stakes game?"

"The very high stakes game has no monetary buy-in or prize. Instead, the winner becomes entitled to one or more of the other players taking part in sexual acts of the winner's choosing, and the other player or players must oblige – right here, tonight," he replies, incongruously calmly and expressionless.

You're completely stunned but you put on your best poker face to try to conceal it from the five men that have their gaze firmly fixed on you, intrigued to see your reaction. You sit there silently, contemplating the options available to you, sometimes trying to avoid eye contact with the men so as to think clearly without feeling pressure and sometimes looking at them to try and get a read on what's going through their minds.

Eventually, you opt to ask a couple of questions to assist your decision-making: "At what point does the winner specify what sexual acts they want and from whom?"

"Before the game commences. We think it adds to the excitement, knowing what's to come – so to speak," the guy from the bar answers, a slight grin spreading across his face as he does so.

"And are there any limits to what sexual acts can be performed?" you continue.

"As I said before, we play no-limit poker here," he replies.

You again pause to think, this time not trying to avert eye contact but rather looking at each of the men in turn. Your heart and mind are racing. On the one hand, you're thinking this is crazy and you should opt not to take part. On the other, you're thinking this could be incredible and you may never get another chance to do anything like this again – and certainly not with a group of guys that are this attractive. You're not even contemplating the monetary buy-in option.

Eventually, you decide to gamble and announce "I like the sound of the very high stakes game. Count me in." in a calm tone that belies how nervous yet excited you've become.

"Excellent," the guy from the bar says, grabbing the pack of cards that have been sat in the middle of the table and beginning to shuffle. "What would everyone like if they win?" he inquires.

"I want to fuck her on the table while the rest of you jerk off over her," one of the other men says, without hesitation.

Once again, you're stunned but try not to show it. The men all have their eyes fixed on you again, clearly trying to gauge your reaction.

"I want her to suck you all off in turn while I fuck her doggy style," says another of the men.

Your surprise increases and you start to realise a theme of sorts is emerging.

"I want you to fuck her pussy while I fuck her in the ass," one of the other men says, pointing to another of the men as he does so.

"I want to fuck her in the ass while you fuck me in the ass," says another of the men, pointing to another of the men as he does so. You really struggle to contain your surprise at this one.

Everyone else except him now having specified their prize, the guy from the bar turns to you and asks, "What would you like?"

This catches you off guard as your thinking hadn't got this far. You've been so busy trying to take in what you're hearing that you've scarcely had a chance to think about your own prize. From the statements so far you realise there really are no limits to what you can have. You pause to think and compose yourself.

"I want to watch *you two* have sex while *you* massage my breasts, *you* lick me out and *you* fuck me in the ass," you state calmly and assertively, turning your head to each of the men respectively as you refer to them and what you'd like them to do.

The men are surprised and impressed in equal measure by your response but now it's their turn to put on their best poker faces so as to not show it.

One of them, though, can't resist a jibe: "Ah, lick her in the front, poke her in the rear!" he says with a smirk. The others remain silent but also can't help but emit slight smirks of their own.

"What about you?" one of the men asks the guy from the bar.

"As it's her first time I want her to get acquainted with all of us. I want her to have sex with all of us, taking each of us in turn and as many of us at the same time as she can handle," the guy from the bar replies.

You've been stunned on a few occasions already but this completely takes your breath away and you can't help but cough a little to recover it.

Pretending not to notice, the guy from the bar asks "Shall we begin?"

You're still recovering from the shock as the other men nod and vocalise their agreement. The guy from the bar starts dealing and the game begins. You fold your first hand pre-flop – the 2-7 off-suit not helping the nerves that you're feeling. You fold the next hand pre-flop as well and the nerves increase a little.

But the third pot brings you better cards – a pair of jacks in the hole. You raise three and a half times the big blind – enough to make it worthwhile but sufficiently cheap as to entice one of the men to call.

Your first flop brings three undercards of different suits. Wasting little time, you bet – again strongly but not so strongly as to scare off your opponent. The man quickly calls. The turn brings another undercard. Again you bet and again the man calls. The river brings another jack. You pause to contemplate how to play what you know to be the nuts. You bet, more strongly this time.

The man pauses to contemplate, staring at you for a while as he does so. Eventually, he opts to call and there's a showdown. You reveal your two jacks/three of a kind and he reveals his cards – two pairs. "Oh, nice hand," he says, as the chips in the middle are passed your way.

"Two jacks in the hole and two pairs – a sign of things to come perhaps?!" another of the men says, half-jokingly and half-seriously, with a smirk.

Winning your first pot relaxes you and for a short while you forget about what may be to follow. The game continues. Almost an hour goes by before one of the men is eliminated, blinded out after a series of poor hands. Another follows soon after. And then another, leaving you, the guy from the bar and one of the other men left with broadly equal stacks.

There are several more hands where there's little action of note, but then the biggest pot of the night so far comes with the guy from the bar hitting a full house on the flop and the other man landing a flush. A series of raises and re-raises leaves them both all-in. The turn and the river are no help to the other man and he's eliminated, leaving you and the guy from the bar heads-up, him with a roughly 2:1 chip lead.

You take a deep breath and try not to think too much about what may be to follow as the next hand is dealt. A number of heads-up pots go by with little action, you winning a few small pots and him likewise.

But then you check your hole cards at the start of the next pot and find a pair of aces. You pause to contemplate how to play such a big hand before opting to raise. He calls and the flop brings another ace. He's first to act and bets. You opt to raise. To your surprise and relish, he calls. You're sure you're well ahead.

The turn brings another ace. You struggle to contain your excitement but just about manage to maintain a calm exterior. To your relish, he once again bets, strongly. You pause to consider your move in an attempt to hide the strength of your hand. This time you just call to try and hint at weakness.

The river arrives and it's the ten of hearts – no cause for concern. The guy from the bar is unmoved for what feels like an eternity. Then he calmly announces, "All in." You can't believe your luck and immediately call, certain that you've doubled your stack.

He turns over his cards. He reveals a king and queen of hearts. You look at the community cards: Alongside the ace of clubs and ace of hearts that have given you four of a kind, and the ten of hearts on the river, the flop brought a jack of hearts. Royal flush! You lost! How did this happen?!

You gulp as the shock hits you and your eyes virtually pop out of your head. It almost feels as though your heart has stopped beating. You slowly drag your gaze away from the community cards and look up to see the five men all fixated on you once again.

There's another silence until one of the men breaks it by saying, "I guess we're all in now," with no suggestion on his face of this being a joke.

"Four aces wasn't good enough. Time to see how you deal with five," says another of the men, looking right into your eyes as he says it.

With that, the five men all get up from their seats and walk around to you. Your heart is beating again but incredibly fast. The adrenaline is flying through your veins. You're full of nerves about what will come next.

But you're pleasantly surprised when all that comes initially is the sensation of one of the men softly kissing you on one side of your neck. And then another of the men kissing you on the other side. Then the guy from the bar moves round in front of you, stoops and starts to kiss you on the lips. Relaxing a little, you start to kiss him back. The soft, gentle kissing from the three men continues for some time, and you start to fully relax and enjoy it.

Eventually, while continuing to kiss you, the guy from the bar starts to slowly undo the buttons on the trouser suit jacket you're wearing. Once all the buttons are undone, he slowly peels off your jacket, with the two men continuing to kiss your neck assisting.

With this, it hits you that things just got real! You feel the nerves and adrenaline return a little. But there's no turning back now, you're pot-committed. Removing the jacket exposes more of your skin – you're only wearing a low-cut top underneath. The two men start kissing you on the newly-exposed skin at the top of your back and down your arms. And then the guy from the bar finally drags his lips from yours and starts kissing the front of your neck and shoulders, and then down towards the top, uncovered part of your breasts.

This is lovely, you think – you weren't expecting this! You relax and enjoy the kissing once again. It's not long before the three men together start to take off your top. Your bra quickly follows. The three men continue to kiss you, between them working their way down your breasts, abdomen and back. As they do so, you feel the guy from the bar start to undo your trousers, and then slowly peel them off to reveal the sexy lingerie you're wearing underneath.

Then you feel his lips start to press against your inner thighs. At this point you notice your pussy start to tingle and moisten, especially when you feel his breath pass over your crotch. After a couple of minutes of slowly, softly kissing around your underwear, he pulls it down carefully, his head going with it, leaving you sat naked on the leather chair.

He then kisses all the way up your inner leg as he comes back up. He pauses just before your pussy. He stays there motionless for a few seconds to tease you. Then he moves in to kiss your pussy for the first time, so faintly it wouldn't be noticeable if you weren't by now so aroused. He kisses it again, and again, a little less gently each time.

He continues kissing your pussy for a while. But then he abruptly stops, grabs you by your hips and pulls you out of your chair towards him so you're stood up with your pussy right in his face.

One of the other men that's been continuing to kiss your back then pulls your chair away and puts his hands firmly on your back, causing you to fall forward. You use your arms to break your fall and suddenly you're bent over the poker table, leaning on your arms, but still with the guy from the bar's face planted in your crotch.

For the first time you start to feel his tongue on your pussy. He starts slowly sliding it all over as if to take in as much of it as he can. As he does so, you feel something press up against your asshole. You can feel it's the erection of one of the men that's been kissing you from behind. Before you know it, he's inserting his cock into your ass. You let out a slight moan as he does so.

As the guy from the bar continues to slide his tongue over your pussy from below, the other man starts thrusting into your ass. Then you feel the hands of the other man that's been kissing you start fondling your breasts.

You're scarcely able to focus on anything else as you stand there, bent over the table, having your breasts fondled and being licked in the front and poked in the rear. But then you notice that at the opposite end of the table, the two other guys who weren't kissing you before are staring back at you, naked. One is bent over the table being fucked in the ass just like you.

As you continue to be indulged by the three men on your side of the table, you can't help but watch the two guys opposite getting it on; for you it's like watching yourself be fucked in a mirror, except there are two hot guys staring back at you and you're getting licked out and having your breasts caressed as well. It turns you on massively.

Suddenly you realise this is exactly the scenario you had asked for if you won the game. Your focus on the sex waivers slightly as you comprehend this.

"How come I'm getting what I asked for?" you mutter, breathlessly.

"I told you we play differently. Here everyone's a winner," the guy from the bar responds, briefly stopping licking you out so as to do so.

Your curiosity satiated, your focus returns to the physicality and you start to moan with pleasure as the oral, anal and breast stimulation you're getting feels incredible, and the guy-on-guy action you're watching at the same time turns you on.

You can feel the man in your ass getting harder, completely filling it, and he lets out sporadic grunts as he thrusts into you, clearly having the time of his life inside you. This turns you on more.

By now, the guy from the bar is focussing his tongue predominantly on your clit, the warm moisture caressing it. It feels divine. The combination of these three men indulging you and you seeing the two men opposite fucking drives you wild, so much so you can feel yourself start getting close to orgasm.

You're now moaning with pleasure on a regular basis. The man fucking you in the ass continues to grunt as he does so and the two men opposite are both also grunting repeatedly as one does the other up the ass while watching you.

The pleasure you're getting, combined with the witnessing of the show unfolding on the opposite side of the table, becomes too much for you to handle. "Yes, yes, YES," you shriek as you climax.

"Oh yeah, that's it baby," the man screwing you in the ass murmurs as you do so, feeling your body convulse from within and your ass tighten around his rock-hard dick.

When your orgasm eventually subsides, the guy from the bar removes his face from your pussy and the man that's been screwing you in the ass slowly withdraws.

"Now it's time to claim my prize," the guy from the bar says.

He lifts your arms up off the table on which you've been leant such that momentarily you're stood up straight (albeit with a little post-orgasmic dizziness). He then turns you around 180 degrees so you're facing him before lifting you up and laying you down on the poker table, your legs dangling off the side. You watch him intently as he does so, wondering (excitedly after what's gone before) what's coming next.

He grabs your legs, pulls them apart and wastes no time inserting his erect cock into your soaking wet pussy. He begins thrusting into you, relatively slowly albeit deeply from the outset, while holding your legs. His eyes are fixated on yours as he does so, trying to get a read on how it feels for you.

After a couple of minutes of this slow but deep thrusting, he starts to penetrate you harder and faster, still watching you intently as he does so.

After a couple more minutes of him fucking you like this, out of the blue he stops and withdraws from you. He steps back away from you and the table you're laid on. Immediately, his place is filled by one of the other men who slides his hard cock into you and begins to screw you, hard and fast from the outset. As he does so, you notice out of the corner of your eyes that all the other guys are now stood around the table naked watching you be fucked while masturbating. Initially, you merely find this arousing, but then it dawns on you that the first of the men to state his desired prize is now claiming it. It causes you to wonder while you continue to be fucked hard and fast whether you're soon going to be showered in four men's spunk.

You don't have to wait long for your answer. After about five minutes of pounding your pussy, the first man to state his desired prize pulls out of you. As he does so, the other four men stop jerking off.

One of them walks round to the edge of the table where you're still laid. He jumps on top of you and quite aggressively turns you over, then lifts you up on to your knees so you're on the table on all fours. He kneels behind you and then you feel his dick enter you.

As he begins to ride you from behind, one of the other men clambers up on to the table and kneels in front of you, his erection drooped in front of your face. You quickly realise what this means – you need to suck it because this is the second man's desired prize. You duly oblige.

You never thought you'd get spit-roasted on a poker table but it feels great! You feel both men's cocks in you get harder from the sucking and fucking action. But just when you think the man in your mouth is about to explode in you, he pulls away and climbs down off the table.

In his place jumps one of the other men that's been stood beside the table waiting, watching. Of course – the second man to state his desired prize wanted you to suck all the other men off while he fucks you doggy style, you remember!

You duly oblige once again. And once again, after pleasuring him for a few minutes with the best technique you can supply while being fucked from behind, just as you think the man in your mouth is about to blow his load in you, he pulls out and climbs down off the table.

This pattern of events continues with the other two men whose cocks you haven't yet sucked and whose dick isn't already thrusting into your pussy. But when the fourth man pulls out of your mouth, the man that's been doing you doggy style also withdraws.

There's no let up in the action though: One of the men leaps back on to the table and slides himself underneath you such that you find yourself face-to-face with him as you remain on all fours. He puts his hands on your hips and pulls your body down so you're lying right on top of him. He inserts his dick into your wet pussy and starts thrusting into you.

Seconds later, one of the other men leaps up to join you on the table. You realise what's coming – the third man to state his desired prize wanted to fuck your ass while the other man fucks your pussy. Sure enough, you feel your ass being penetrated by hard cock again. And then you feel the weight of the man that's just entered on top of you as he lies down on you, leaving you completely sandwiched. They both thrust into you, once again vigorously from the get-go.

Being double-teamed hard and fast by these men, their bodies pressed up against yours and their breath on you, feels thrilling. You can't help but let out sporadic moans as they do so.

The sandwich continues for several minutes, although you're so lost in the excitement and pleasure that it could be hours for all you know. But then the man under you stops thrusting into your pussy, pushes your body up off him ever so slightly, withdraws from you and carefully slides back out from underneath you.

There's no let up from the man in your ass though. Without removing his dick from you, he pushes you down so you're flat on the table and he's fully laid on top of you. He continues thrusting into you.

But then you hear him groan right into your ear and feel extra weight on top of you. Another of the men has just mounted the man fucking you and started fucking his ass at the same time – it's the fourth man to state his desired prize claiming it, you realise! This is amazing –

I've never been involved in a threesome like this before, you think to yourself!

The man inside you starts to groan with pleasure repeatedly right in your ear as he rides you and gets ridden himself. Again, this three-way anal action lasts for a few minutes but you've lost all concept of time as you're enjoying yourself so much.

Eventually, you feel the weight on top of you lighten; the man on top of you both has withdrawn from the ass of the man directly on top of you and climbed down off the table. And then you feel the dick you've had pummelling your ass for so long now withdraw from you, and the man lifts himself off you and follows the other man off the table.

You continue to lay there face down on the poker table, unsure what's coming next. You feel hands on your hips and you're turned on to your back. The guy from the bar is knelt upright in front of you on the table. He picks you up off the baize and pulls you on top of him, his arms around your waist. You put your arms around him to hold on to him.

He then inserts his dick into your pussy and begins thrusting into you. As he does so, with you suspended in mid-air wrapped around him, one of the other men climbs back on to the table and lays down on his back in the middle of it. The guy from the bar then stops thrusting into you and leans forward, taking you with him. You land on top of the man laid out on the table and the guy from the bar lands on top of you, his dick still deep inside you. And then yet again you feel hard cock enter your ass, as the man underneath you penetrates you.

The two of them start double-teaming you in the middle of the table. Then the three of you are joined by one of the other men. He kneels upright on one side of the latest sandwich, and dangles his cock in your face, carefully manoeuvring it towards you without touching the men as they bang you.

You know what you have to do! Somewhat difficult though it is while you're being double-teamed, you turn your head towards the man's cock and use one of your hands to grab it and pull it towards your mouth. You open your mouth, take him inside you and do your best to suck him while being jerked around by the double-fucking you're getting from the men above and below you.

Just as you get used to having three men in you at once, the other two climb back up on to the table and move towards you on either side, also both kneeling upright. One of them grabs your free hand, places it against his erection and then wraps your fingers around it. The other carefully peels your other hand away from the man you're sucking's cock and likewise places it around his.

It's clear you have to jerk them off, and as you start to do so you realise this is the guy from the bar claiming the rest of his prize – all the guys have taken their turn with you and now it's time for you to take them all at once.

This provides you with added motivation to jerk off and suck off the three men while your pussy and ass are fucked by the guy from the bar and the other man, respectively. Consequently, you do your best to concentrate on the three men knelt either side of you and give them your best hand and blow job technique.

But it's so difficult when you're getting double-teamed by the other two men, and it only gets harder as the three men you're sucking and jerking off start to use their hands to fondle the parts of your hot naked body they can reach from where they're knelt – the additional stimulation adding to your pleasure and distracting you from your sucking and jerking.

The stimulation you're now getting from all sides feels incredible – it feels as though your whole body is being stimulated, internally as well as externally. You'd moan over and over with pleasure if you could but the cock-sucking you're doing prevents it.

The men are all grunting and groaning as you simultaneously pleasure them all, though, and this adds to your arousal. You feel their dicks all getting even harder in your hands, mouth, pussy and ass.

And then the next thing you know, a finger touches your clit. You have no idea whose hand it is nor how it got there because you're so lost with all the other action and stimulation but you sure as hell don't care! The finger starts stroking your clit and this tips you over the edge. Your body goes into overwhelming ecstasy and your eyes almost pop out of your head as you have the most mind-blowing orgasm.

The other men, whose dicks are all now throbbing from the pleasure you're giving them, see and feel this and this sends them over the edge: first the man in your mouth, whose cock you struggle to continue sucking as you climax, explodes in your mouth; then you feel your ass flood with the cum of the man who's fucking it; then you feel the spunk of the two men you've been wanking spurt over your face, neck and breasts; and then finally, the guy from the bar orgasms and sheds his load into your pussy.

They all simultaneously let out a final roar of pleasure as they cum, and both their roars and the feeling of their spunk ejaculate into you and all over you provides even greater stimulation for you and makes the final stages of your already out-of-this-world orgasm even more unbelievable. You never want this to end.

But like all good things it has to. One by one your orgasms start to subside. Initially, none of you move. But then the man with his cock in your mouth withdraws it and slowly and carefully manoeuvres himself away and off the table. You take this as your cue to unclasp your hands from the two men you've jerked off and whose dicks are now starting to go flaccid. Now freed, they too slowly and carefully move away and off the table.

Then the man with his cock in your ass slowly withdraws, leaving just the guy from the bar still inside you. Still lying on top of you, he looks you in the eyes, freshly re-opened after being closed for the majority of your orgasm, and asks, "Anyone up for another game?"

A South African Adventure (1)

You and your man are on holiday in South Africa, flying into Cape Town and then touring through the winelands and along the Garden Route to Johannesburg via Lesotho. One of the stops on the Garden Route is at a great place on a cliff overlooking the beautiful bay outside. The room you're staying in is large, with floor-to-ceiling windows all along the side of the property overlooking the bay. The day you're spending here coincides with his birthday.

He wakes up in the morning and opens the blinds. To his amazement, a huge pod of dolphins is swimming past parallel to the coast no more than about one hundred metres from the shore. He gets back into bed and watches them flying through the air and sea from one side of the bay to the other until they eventually disappear out of sight. That in itself could possibly be the most incredible start to any day, never mind a birthday. Except that it transpires that this is just the start...

You're there in bed with him, completely naked from having welcomed in his birthday with a night of passion – one of those sessions that ends up with both of you exhausted and sweaty but thoroughly satisfied to the point you both just immediately fall asleep afterwards in the early hours.

Him opening the blinds and letting the sunshine in causes you to stir from your slumber. Initially, he just leaves you to adjust your bleary eyes to the incredible vista and enjoy the dolphins (when you're awake enough to realise that's what you've woken up to), that are now flying back past the other way across the bay.

But he's already seen this spectacle and by now he's enjoying a different view: After a few minutes he decides the sight of your gorgeous body in all its glory is too much to leave alone, so as you lie there on your side, gazing out of the huge windows to the bay where the dolphins continue to swim through, he moves his body up close to you and starts softly stroking you and gently kissing your neck and back.

Initially, you just smile but don't really flinch because you're still enjoying the incredible scene outside. But then you feel one of his arms around you, holding you close while he continues to gently caress your body with the other.

Now right up against you, you feel his cock press up against you as it starts to throb, and you start to get distracted from the outside world. With one arm around you, holding you against him, and him continuing to gently kiss you, his free hand, having repeatedly gently stroked every other part of your body, eventually slides up your leg and stops.

His fingers start to gently caress your pussy. You start to quietly moan with pleasure. He starts to stroke you a little faster and your clit fully emerges. You start to moan more loudly and regularly. You feel yourself get wetter and wetter.

You're now so lost in the pleasure that you put your hand on his bottom and push him towards you. You're so wet and he's so hard that his cock glides into you. At which point you let out an extra loud moan of pleasure.

He starts to slowly thrust in and out of you, one arm still wrapped around you, the fingers of the other still caressing your pussy. You're now moaning loudly and regularly, causing him to start to thrust faster and harder, all the while continuing to stroke your pussy.

The pleasure is now so intense – it feels so good with your bodies entwined, him continuing to kiss your neck and stroke your pussy whilst his rock-hard cock thrusts deep inside you. And you can't do anything but just scream as your body goes into seizure as you climax. And as he sees, hears and feels you orgasm, this sends him over the edge and he lets out a roar right into your ear as he explodes inside of you.

As the stroking, kissing and thrusting slows, the orgasm passes and the post-coital smiles start to appear. Your gazes return to the ocean outside and you notice that the dolphins have gone but you're both left with the feeling that the most incredible day is just beginning.

A South African Adventure (2)

So, there you are, lying in bed, naked, feeling elated after the unique sight of the dolphin pod and the early morning pleasure that you shared, with the sunshine beating in and the brilliant blue of the sky and the ocean surrounding you.

He certainly doesn't want to waste the day (it being his birthday and you being free to do whatever you want), but a big part of him also wants to take a little bit of time to just enjoy the moment. So initially he just lies there looking at you, faintly stroking the skin all over your body again, while inhaling your scent with every breath he takes.

He does this for a few minutes before deciding that the icing on the cake of this already-fantastic moment would be to add some champagne to the equation. He grabs a bottle from the fridge, together with a couple of flutes, and brings them back to bed, where you still are, looking divine in your birthday suit, and now with an even bigger post-coital smile on your face.

He pops the cork and pours you both a glass in a metaphoric reminder of the way he exploded inside you a short while earlier. You then proceed to just lie there, each with one arm around the other whilst sipping champagne with your free arm, enjoying the vista around you, the taste of the bubbles and the touch of the other's body.

You continue like this for a little while, him topping you up regularly as the flutes start to empty. But then the serenity is broken a little when you somewhat suddenly turn your head and look directly at him. The thoughtful look on your face combined with the glint in your eye tells him an idea has come into your mind and you want to explore it.

Still holding your now half-full glass of champagne, you shuffle down the bed a little and start softly kissing his chest. You carry on kissing him as you ever-so-slowly shimmy down the bed further, your lips pressing against his abs, then his nave and then the top of his thighs.

You then notice that a big erection is knocking against your face, pulsing every time you kiss another part of his skin. You stop briefly to take a mouthful of champagne. Then you grab his erection and put it in your mouth to join the bubbles inside. Initially you just wait there, letting him get used to the beautiful sensation of the combination of the warm moisture of your mouth and the fizz of the champagne. Then you start sliding your mouth up and down his cock, really slowly so as to not lose the mouthful of champagne, keeping your eyes on him the whole time so as to see how much pleasure you're giving him.

You keep going like this for a couple of minutes until he's absolutely rock-solid, throbbing in your mouth, and the fizz of the champagne starts to make way for your saliva. You stop sliding your mouth up and down his cock, swallow and take him out of your mouth. You then hitch yourself up on top of him so you're straddling him with his solid cock nestled against your pussy, never taking your eyes off him and him never taking his eyes off you.

You grab the champagne bottle and slowly pour most of what's left of it over your breasts, using your hands to rub a little of it more widely over them but letting the rest trickle down your body and on to your touching love organs.

As you feel the trickle reach your inner thigh and pussy, you take your hand and slowly massage the champagne all around your pussy, using your fingertips to insert a little into your vagina. As you and he both start to feel a tingle from the fizz on your respective pleasure zones, you lift up slightly and place his tingling, throbbing cock inside you.

Your eyes are still transfixed on one another as you start riding him, slowly at first and then gradually a little faster and deeper as you get used to having him inside you once again. You keep riding him and he feels more of your juices releasing around his cock, which in turn turns him on and makes him even harder.

As you look into each other's eyes while you ride him, you can see he's in heaven. This prompts a faint smile – a combination of naughty, happy and in pleasure – to appear on your face. It stays there as you continue to ride him.

You then start to slow down and eventually bring your riding to a halt. He's mystified as you lift up and take him out of you but continue to straddle him. You keep your gaze firmly fixed on him, still with that naughty smile on your face, as you grab the champagne bottle once again and proceed to pour the rest of the champagne directly over his cock.

Before the champagne has a chance to slide down off his cock, you adjust your straddle position ever so slightly and then lower yourself back on to him – except this time he can feel it's your ass you've placed him in.

You start to gently ride him again, his fizzing cock sliding in and out of your tight ass. As you carry on riding him, still looking straight into his eyes with that naughty grin on your face, you softly ask, "How does that feel?... You like that?" knowing full well from the look on his face that he's in absolute ecstasy.

The talking turns him on even more and you feel him get even harder in your ass. You carry on riding him and, now knowing that the talking turns him on too, you say, "Ooh someone's getting harder... I guess you do like that."

You feel his cock get harder still as you say it, and you can tell from the feeling of it in your ass, the look on his face and the way his body is starting to tense that he's close to orgasm, so you place one of your hands on your clit and start stroking yourself.

"It feels like someone wants to cum in my ass," you say, stating the obvious to try and arouse him further, still with your gaze fixated on him as you stroke yourself and ride him. "Do you?... Do you want to cum in my tight little ass?... Do it... Do it... Cum in my ass... I want your spunk in my ass... Give it to me... Cum in my ass!"

You staring into his eyes with a naughty grin on your face as you ride him with your ass and talk dirty to him, all whilst pleasuring yourself with your fingers, is just too much for him to take: He does exactly what you say and lets out a huge roar of pleasure as he explodes in your ass. And you seeing, hearing and feeling this whilst touching yourself is enough to send you over the edge – you howl as you climax whilst sitting on his dick.

As your respective orgasms subside, he's left trying to comprehend what's just happened. After a couple of minutes, still inside your ass and somewhat breathless but now just about able to speak as you look back at him, now with a big beaming smile on your face which represents a combination of sexual fulfilment and satisfaction of what you've just achieved with him, he asks, "What was that in aid of?"

After a slight pause, you reply, "You go out of your way to give me as much pleasure as you possibly can all the rest of the time so, as it's your birthday, I wanted to do something special to repay the favour." With that, a big smile appears across his face – he now knows that, even though it's still only the morning, it's already the best birthday ever.

A South African Adventure (3)

After a brief period of just staying as you are, you straddling him and him lying there still trying to comprehend quite what's just happened, eventually you lift yourself off him and walk over to the phone in the room – partly so as to call room service to request some sustenance after the morning's sexploits and partly to show off your peachy ass as a further reminder of what you've just done for/to him.

A tray of delicious breakfast treats soon arrives and you momentarily put on a robe to open the door and take in the tray but then immediately discard it again as soon as the door is closed. You go out onto your secluded balcony with the tray, and for the first time today get to breathe in the fresh seaside air and properly feel the sun on your naked skin.

You sit there facing each other, admiring the view of both each other in all your glory and the beautiful ocean vista whilst nibbling on the treats that have just arrived. There's not much conversation as he's still replaying and trying to take in the events of the morning so far in his mind while eating and looking at you and the scenery. He has absolutely no problem just relaxing and really taking his time with breakfast on the balcony in these environs having had such an incredible morning already.

Eventually, when you both decide you've had enough to eat, you agree that it's about time you go and do something outside of your accommodation. Part of him doesn't even want to shower because he's loving having your scent, taste and the residue of your bodily fluids (and champagne) all over him. But you take a shower together and then for the first time get dressed and make your way outside.

It's now about eleven-thirty a.m. and, before the safari at dusk, you've booked an afternoon wine-tasting at a glorious estate in the hills a few miles away from the coast where you're staying. As it's such a beautiful day and location, and still comparatively early, you decide to take a gentle stroll there rather than take transport.

As you slowly ascend away from the coast, the sea starts to become more of a distant view behind you and the lush grass of the hills becomes the dominant view in front and around. Although the hills and greenery remind you of home, the clear blue sky, the now-hot sunshine and the plants and creatures you encounter are anything but.

As you ascend further, vineyards start to appear on the horizon. Eventually, you reach your destination, a beautiful estate in acres of meticulously landscaped grounds, which are themselves surrounded by acres and acres of vineyards, with the sea still visible on one side in the distance, down below.

As you arrive for your one p.m. booking, you're greeted by a host who, after completing formalities, escorts you to a large table outside on the beautifully maintained lawns, which is strategically placed so as to allow the guests to either sit themselves on an unshaded side of the table or on a side of the table that is offered protection from the sun by the branches of a vast, old tree.

You take your seats at the table. There are already a couple of other guests sat at the table, enjoying glasses of wine. You acquaint yourselves with them before the host returns with a glass for each of you. The host explains the background to this first wine, a chenin blanc, the grapes that are used to create it, the soil that's required and the notes that you'll experience when you try it. The host then leaves you be and you take your first sip.

It's very good. You both remark as such and the other guests comment likewise. You proceed to engage in light conversation with your new compatriots whilst sipping on the gorgeous wine and enjoying the sun and surroundings. A couple more guests join and you all again acquaint yourselves as this time they get the introduction from the host.

As each of the guests' glasses start to empty, the host returns with a new glass of wine, a pinotage, and accompanying explanation. You both continue to relax in this serene environment, enjoying the wine, conversation and views for quite some time.

Then a couple more people are escorted to your table, this time a couple of ladies who look to be in their late twenties or early thirties, both chatting away as they walk to the table with big grins on their face, evidently looking forward to a great afternoon ahead.

You're both distracted from your drinking and conversation by their arrival, initially by the noise of their chatting and laughing as they walk towards the table but latterly by one of them in particular whose appearance is striking. She's a beautiful woman but there's something else about her that's striking – something in the way she walks and other subtleties that neither of you can quite put your finger on.

Neither of you initially notices that the other has subconsciously found themselves looking at her but then you both look at each other and realise that you both were. Your gaze pauses on each other and you subliminally communicate to each other that you know the other has clocked her and has noticed that there's something about her. You exchange smiles as a result and take a knowing sip of your wine.

The two ladies join you at the table, taking a seat next to you, and again everyone acquaints themselves as the two new arrivals receive their first glass of wine and you both take another sip of your third.

Very quickly, your initial sense of there being something about one of the new joiners is confirmed as, after the initial small talk is out of the way, following her first sip of wine she remarks, "Ohh that is so good. That is the best thing I've ingested since the last time my ex did me from behind before he started using and couldn't get it up any more."

Everyone at the table laughs a little, takes a sip of their respective wines and then returns to conversation. As the conversation and wine-tasting continues, the discourse inevitably splits geographically and the two of you end up engaging singularly with the two ladies sat next to you.

You instantly hit it off with the latest attendees, who it transpires are long-time friends that decided to take a holiday together after having both come out of long-term relationships within the space of three months. There's a chemistry that sees the conversation quickly take a raunchy turn alongside a lot of laughs – and imbibing of beautiful wines. But the connection is definitely stronger with the striking woman, who is more vocal.

The conversations going on at the two ends of the table get noisier as the time rolls by and the guests get tipsier. At your end of the table, the body language of the striking woman gets more flirty and she starts asking you both some quite intimate questions, albeit in a light-hearted manner.

Eventually, after a couple of hours at the table, the host comes over to the table for a final time to announce that your wine-tasting has come to an end but that if you want to you can stay at the table for a little longer or take a walk around the grounds.

You look at each other and then the ladies next to you. The striking lady looks at you and says, "Shall we go for a walk around the grounds?" You agree to this but the quieter, less flirty lady says that she'll stay at the table and just enjoy the sunshine.

The three of you start slowly strolling around the grounds. There's not much conversation other than remarks about how beautiful the grounds are. After a few minutes you arrive at an area with a sign at the entrance saying 'Good-time Gardens'. By this time, you've walked far enough as to be well out of sight of everyone else and even the grand main building is quite distant.

You wonder into the gardens. They're full of an array of plants and bushes, a mix of vibrant colours and scents, and flanked on all sides by immaculately maintained hedges. After ambling around the gardens for about a minute, you stumble upon a small area that consists of just a bench surrounded by a small patch of grass, obviously designed for sitting and contemplating life or reading amongst the flowery surrounds. Your companion stops, turns to you and says, "Wanna have some fun?"

"What kind of fun?" you reply to her, as a faint smile appears on your face. She moves closer to you and softly kisses you on the lips. She then steps away a little but keeps her eyes fixated on you as if quizzically asking you for validation of what she's just done.

You answer her subliminal question by pulling her towards you and starting to snog her. After the best part of a minute, the snogging comes to a natural pause. She slowly pulls back a little, turns to him, grabs him by the collar of his short-sleeve shirt, pulls him towards her and starts snogging him.

Again, the snogging finds a natural pause after about a minute. She takes the opportunity to step back a little once more and this time puts one hand behind each of you and applies pressure so as to push you towards each other, as if she now wants you two to snog. You duly oblige.

Again, after a short period, your snogging comes to a natural pause. When it does, this time she pulls you towards her, starts snogging you and, with one arm, pushes him towards you, as if to say to him, "You join in, let's both play with her."

After what you've already done for him that day, he's more than happy to accede to her implied request. As she snogs you, he starts softly kissing your neck. Both her and his hands start slowly and softly working their way around your upper body and then down to your buttocks and the top of your legs.

This combination of tripartite kissing and petting continues for a few minutes. You notice that you've started to get really moist between your legs and, as if she can tell, just as you notice, she starts lifting up your top. It's a lovely, light, low-cut number that's practical for the hot afternoon sun whilst also sufficiently revealing as to let people know that you've got great assets and you're happy to flaunt them – but not too much so as to ensure that something is left to the imagination.

She lifts your top off and immediately you decide you should reciprocate. Then, as if to let him know he's not being forgotten about, she firmly pulls your man towards her and starts snogging him again, this time starting to unbutton his shirt as their mouths entwine. Once all the buttons are undone, she peels off his shirt, still snogging him in the process. She proceeds to take off her own bra and then reaches for yours, whilst still snogging him.

With all of you now topless, she stops snogging him, takes one of your hands in each of hers and slowly pulls you both towards the small, neat patch of grass, where she lies herself down, pulling you both down with her, as if to say, "Now it's time for you two to play with me for a bit."

You both start softly kissing parts of her soft skin. There's not really enough room for both your heads on her upper body though so, while you continue to kiss her breasts and abdomen, he starts kissing her legs, which are bare because of the short shorts she's wearing.

As you continue to kiss her, you unbutton her shorts and then he pulls them off to reveal a tiny red G-string. Your lips wander towards it and, as they do, she lets out a soft moan. You continue to softly kiss her there but after a couple of minutes she, somewhat unexpectedly, pushes you away and gently rolls you onto your back.

From his vantage point of her lower legs, he surmises that she's probably decided that she's enjoying herself so much but doesn't want to peak too soon nor perhaps be too selfish and hog all the attention for too long.

She rolls on top of you, whilst simultaneously grabbing him and pulling him towards her. She starts kissing your breasts and at the same time slides her fingers up your leg and up the short skirt you're wearing until she reaches your underwear.

He starts kissing her back. She continues kissing you, softly, working her way down your abdomen until she reaches your skirt, whilst at the same time gently stroking you between your legs. She can feel how wet you are through your underwear and decides it's time for your skirt to come off. She lifts up a little to enable herself to pull it down and momentarily locks eyes with you as she does it, as if to say to you, "In case you don't know, you're super-hot and I want you."

With your skirt off, she moves her lips to your crotch and at the same time flails her arms out behind her to grab his shorts and start unbuttoning them. She pulls them and his underwear down together while continuing to kiss your crotch. With him now naked, he pulls her G-string down and at the same time she pulls your thong down. She then really dives into your pussy with her mouth and starts to slide her tongue around it.

With you laid out, legs spread and her tongue teasing you, she turns her body a full 180 degrees so her pussy is straddling your face, inviting you to reciprocate – which you do. With you both eating each other out, she reaches out a hand to him and pulls him towards the end where your face and her pussy meet.

She pulls him around to behind her, grabs his cock and pulls it towards her pussy. She proceeds to place him inside her with your tongue just millimetres away, now fixated on her clitoris. He starts to thrust in to her and, as he does so, she lets out a moan into your pussy.

The sound and the vibration of the moan both stimulate you and turn you on in equal measure. He thrusts in and out of her, his balls gently slapping into your face in the process. He can feel your breath on his shaft and balls as you lick her out. Her tongue feels amazing but being able to pleasure her at the same time and get an ultra-close-up view of him fucking her turns you on almost as much. The combination causes you to let out a moan as well, which he can feel as he thrusts into her.

As he thrusts faster and deeper into her, she starts to moan more loudly and more frequently, and it becomes clear your companion is someone who gets off from penetration. It's not long before her moaning turns to a shriek and her body tenses as she climaxes.

You both feel a squirt of fluid emerge from inside her, partly on to his balls and partly on to your face. This surprise only serves to turn you both on more and your respective moans tell her that she should continue licking you out and allowing him to fuck her.

With her staying where she is, he does likewise. It's not long before her moaning returns, getting louder and louder almost with every thrust of his cock and flick of your tongue. You're totally turned on by it, not to mention in heaven with the pleasure she's giving you. You're all now moaning with pleasure, almost in unison, but then another shriek emerges as she climaxes again. This time, though, this brings you to orgasm.

He continues to thrust in and out of her, having the time of his life as he hears, sees and feels you both orgasm together. He could easily explode as well in the midst of this but does everything he can to hold himself back because he doesn't want this to end yet.

As your orgasm subsides, he pulls out of her and pulls her off you. He decides it's time for you to get double the pleasure. He lies down and pulls you on to him so that you're once again straddling him, just as you had been hours before. He then pulls her butt towards his face. She lies down on top of him such that her pussy rests in his face and her face is on your pussy.

You start riding him, he starts licking her and she tries to keep her tongue on your clit as you gyrate on his cock. Now it's your turn to have the heavenly view of two people pleasuring you – and each other – all while the hot sunshine beats down on your skin.

She starts moaning again as his tongue slides over her clit. As do you as her tongue does likewise on yours and you feel his throbbing cock inside you. As does he as you start to ride him faster and he gets more turned on by the intoxicating scent of her soaking wet pussy in his face.

This train of pleasure continues, getting more intense with every lick and ride. The moans get louder and more frequent as each of you pleasures each other more and more. She hears your moans start to get really loud and with one of her spare hands decides to reach round and put a finger in your ass.

You've now got his cock in one hole, her finger in another and her tongue sliding over your clit. As well as the pleasure you're giving him as you ride him, he can now feel her hand on his balls as she thrusts her finger into your ass. This extra stimulation for both of you is too much and sends you and him both over the edge at the same time. This in turn sends her over the edge for a third time, and as his spunk fires into you, he feels a squirt from her all over his face.

As the orgasms subside, you slowly peel yourselves apart – her removing her finger from you, you lifting off him and then her doing likewise. You all stand up, and for a few moments just hold your stances, silent, looking at each other as you recover your breath and enjoy the sun on your skin.

You all start to smile as the comprehension of what you've just done seeps in. Eventually, you say, "Well, I guess we'd better make our way back." They both smile and agree, and you all proceed to recover your clothes from the various parts of the 'Good-time Garden' to which they've been flung.

Even though you're all filthy, covered in each other's juices, none of you minds and you put your clothes on irrespective. You walk back to the table, where you find your striking companion's friend fast asleep.

He looks at the time and sees it's four p.m. With your safari booked to start at four-thirty p.m., he walks off to arrange a taxi. You ask your very satisfied companion where she's staying and the sound of your voice wakes her friend from her slumber. He returns and you make your excuses and head off to begin the next chapter in today's adventure, still tingling from the pleasure of the last.

A South African Adventure (4)

You return from the safari, having been amazed by what you saw and experienced. You decide to relax by the pool for a short while before heading out for the evening. You put your swimming costumes on and head for the infinity pool, which to your surprise is empty. He dives straight into the water whilst you go to lie down on one of the outdoor canopy beds.

Whilst he vigorously swims lengths of the pool, memories of the day's adventures race back into his head. He is having flashbacks of your breasts, cupping them with his hands, pressing himself against you from behind, the smell of your skin, the heavy breathing…

He halts his swimming and comes to the surface as he feels his cock start to harden in his swimming shorts. Then he captures a glimpse of your peachy bum cheeks in the Brazilian bikini you're wearing just a few metres away and decides to get out of the pool and come towards you.

He approaches the head of the bed and, dripping wet, asks you how you're doing. You look up and see his erection bulging out of his swimming shorts. Your eyes cross and lock. He puts his hands on his shorts and slowly pulls them down to let his hard cock bounce out of them.

"I've been missing you in the pool," he says.

You take his cock into your hand and put the tip of it on your lips. He gasps and puts his hand on your cheek. You open your mouth and put his dick on your tongue, rolling it all the way around the tip.

"I've been missing you here on the bed," you break to respond.

You take a big mouthful of his member and he shudders from the sensation but then, to your surprise, he pulls it out of you and goes to the bottom of the bed. You don't know what's going on but then he crawls onto the bed, grabs your ankles, spreads your legs and starts to kiss them with a mischievous look on his face.

Goosebumps appear on your skin, which is getting more and more tender as he moves up your legs. You look around to see if anyone can see you but you can't tell if anyone is around in the fading light and frankly you don't even care – the fact that someone can watch him go down on you turns you on and you arch your back more and more as he starts to lick up your thigh.

When he gets to your bikini bottoms, he firstly starts to rub his tongue and fingers on the material – long strokes up and down, pressing harder each time. His left hand is holding the left side of your body down against the bed so that you have little capacity for movement and have to give in to whatever he is doing.

Your nipples harden as you get more and more aroused. You drive your fingers through his hair and guide his face down towards your clit. He takes the hint and pushes the material to the side. His tongue starts to play with you.

Your body initially shivers as he starts to suck on your clit but after a moment you fully relax into it. You want him to spread your legs wider and for him to finger your ass as he eats you out. He feels your body wanting to move and he spreads your legs wide open. He then licks his fingers and starts to rub them against you, inserting them into you interchangeably as you indulge in the sensation.

But then again he suddenly stops and pulls out. "Shall we go to the pool?" he asks.

Your head is in something of a foggy haze and as you lift your head up you see him diving back into the pool. Not thinking much about it, you undo the top of your bikini, pull your pants down and run to the pool naked. You dive in and emerge on the other side. The sudden wetness and cool of the water is a shock to your body and mind.

He swims towards you and you start goofing around in the pool, just laughing and having fun. "It's been the best birthday I've ever had," he says, all of a sudden. There's a silent pause. Then he puts his hand on your neck, draws you close and kisses you.

The longer you kiss, the more intense it gets, your bodies tightly pressed against each other, and your breathing getting heavy. You jump up and, carried by the water, weightlessly wrap your legs around him. He eases you onto him. You melt into him. He pushes your back against the rim of the pool and kisses your neck as his dick penetrates you into utter submission.

You moan quietly under your breath, aware that you're in a public space. But it's all just too exhilarating and you can't stay quiet as you cum hard and fast. As your body convulses, it pushes him over the edge and he climaxes, wrapped in your embrace.

It now dark, the hotel pool crew emerge from nowhere and, spotting you, ask you to leave the pool area so that it can be cleaned, them almost as embarrassed as you are. You politely oblige.

A South African Adventure (5)

Your soggy bodies, tingling from the ecstasy you've given them, toddle back to your room. You giggle like children about the way you almost got caught indulging in your naughty behaviour on the way. You both remove what little clothing you have on and hop into the shower together.

He washes off the remnants of the day's exquisite events whilst admiring your body in all its glory as the water lashes over it and a beautiful smile looks back at him, contented from the day you've enjoyed together. He toys with having some more fun in the shower – making use of the two showerheads available is very tempting – but ultimately decides to save that for another time.

You get out and get yourselves dressed as you have a dinner reservation at a plush restaurant nearby. Although you don't have to, you make a real effort with yourself, putting on an unbelievable dress, heels, a diamond encrusted necklace and your favourite perfume.

After a short taxi ride, you arrive at the restaurant and are escorted to a gorgeous outdoor bar area where you can get a pre-dinner aperitif. As you walk through the restaurant to the bar, all the other guests turn their heads and look at you – the men lusting after you and the women jealous that they can't look as stunning and that you've stolen their men's attention.

The bar-restaurant is just a couple of miles down the coast from where you're staying. Even though it's night-time, it's still lovely and warm. There's also a full moon, its light causing the sea below to glisten. The bar area is beautifully moody, dimly lit with a candle on each table that sits around the crescent-shaped bar that hangs over the edge of the cliffs. The sound of the waves gently sloshing against the rocks is accompanied by chill-out music and the murmur of the other guests.

As you both gleefully recount the day's events, he can't help but notice how sexily you consume the cocktail you've ordered – the way you slide the decorative cherry off into your mouth and the way you suggestively suckle on the straw are so titillating that part of him already wants to just drag you out of there to the nearest secluded place and just take you there and then. But he restrains himself and just enjoys the discourse, as he's reminded what an incredible day you've already had.

You finish your aperitifs and are escorted to your table in the restaurant, another dimly lit outdoor area hanging over the cliffs. The food is exquisite – three small but perfectly presented courses of divine and diverse but somehow complementary flavours, each perfectly paired with a delicious glass of wine, that leaves you both remarking with almost every bite and sip how good they are.

You eventually settle up and then debate briefly what you should do next; it's still comparatively early and it's a gorgeous evening and location so you decide to go on to another bar a very short walk along the cliff edge from the restaurant. This bar is quite a lot bigger than the previous one, with a much larger outdoor space in particular. It's also a lot livelier, with a hefty crowd already dancing and louder music with a thumping beat pumping out from enormous speakers strategically situated in various corners.

You proceed to get a drink but after only a couple of (seductive) sips you grab his arm and lead him into the crowd on the al fresco dancefloor. You start gyrating your body and he starts to move with you, combining it with the occasional sip of his drink. He can see and feel that you're enjoying the opportunity to shake your body and feel the beat, as well as the energy of the venue more generally.

Gorgeous though you look, here people aren't really noticing you as they're lost in their own revelry, and in some ways it feels as though you're the only people in the place as you grind up against each other.

The dancing continues and you start to really get lost in each other. The way your body rubs against his causes his cock to harden, which in turn arouses you as his erection rubs up against you. You continue to move to the beat, your bodies grinding up against each other and you both getting more and more aroused in the process.

The combination of your dancing, the energy of the crowded venue and balmy evening cause you both to perspire a little – but this just adds to the arousal. As you continue to dance – or what now virtually amounts to mating with your clothes on – amidst the other revellers, his mind starts to race with where to take this next, fighting between his desires to do even more naughty things with you and the thought that you might just want to stay here and prolong this raunchy experience.

Initially reluctant to pull you away from this experience that you seem to be revelling in, he continues to grind up against you, his cock getting harder and harder in the process. But then he feels your thong – you're now so wet that it's flooded and he can even feel it through his (admittedly thin) trousers.

For a brief moment he thinks about unzipping his trousers and penetrating you right there on the dancefloor but he again restrains himself. This time, however, he grabs your hand and leads you away from the dancefloor and very briskly out of the premises completely.

He saw that there was a path running along the cliffs from the bar when you arrived and he starts walking you down this. After just a minute or so, he decides you've gone far enough. Although the music from the bar is still audible, you're far enough away that no-one can see you from it, unless they look closely in the right direction.

His cock is throbbing and it's just desperate to plunge inside you but once again he somehow finds the resolve to restrain himself. He decides that you deserve a treat and instead hitches you up on to the rocks, pulls your dress up and your soaking thong down, and plunges his face into your pussy.

You immediately let out a soft moan at this unexpected development. He, meanwhile, becomes intoxicated in the scent and taste of your pussy – "Oh, you taste and smell so good," he whispers – and also the delight of how unbelievably wet he's made you.

The floods of juices coming out of you provoke him to soon insert his fingers into you while his tongue glides over your clit. This causes you to moan again, this time more loudly, and he takes this as a sign of encouragement to insert a finger in your ass as well.

It's not long before the combined stimulation of your clit, vagina and ass on top of how turned on you already cause you to orgasm intensely. Even though you're in a public place where anyone could come by at any moment, you let out a really loud shriek as you do so. It's only for the borderline deafening music in the bar that the revellers there don't hear you.

On this occasion, hearing, seeing and feeling you climax like that is too much for him to resist and, as soon as you're done, he pulls out his cock and plunges it into you, deep from the very first thrust. With him so unbelievably turned on by everything about you, very quickly he's thrusting furiously into you. Your mouth is wide open and your eyes are bulging as the penetrating you're getting from his throbbing cock is almost too much to handle. It feels incredible and for him it is too much to handle – he lets out an almighty roar as he explodes inside you, the orgasm so intense and seeming to last for an age.

The Scrum

It's Friday night. You've had an intense and stressful week and you're desperate to just let your hair down and forget about all your travails for a few hours. You'd had drinks with a girlfriend diarised for this evening for several weeks and, although you're half-tempted to cancel because you think you won't be much company and aren't even sure you'll be able to make it, you force yourself to shut down your laptop, quickly get dolled up and rush out to meet her.

Despite the rush, you know you're meeting at a popular bar and you want to look good to help you feel better after the tough week so you put on a delicious red dress and take enough time to make sure your make-up leaves your face looking radiant.

On the journey to the bar you're still flustered; you're running late and still thinking about the worst of the matters that have been bothering you during the week. Happily, it doesn't show and to the rest of the underground carriage you're just another gorgeous woman making her way out for a night on the tiles.

You arrive at the bar. It's packed and you have to barge your way through the crowd a little – which doesn't help your mood – before you see your friend sitting alone at a table, sipping on a drink and looking at her phone.

You go over to her and apologise profusely for being late, giving a quick overview of the reasons why in the process. She's completely forgiving and is genuine when she says not to worry but warns you she's on something of a curfew so is going to have to leave within ninety minutes of your arrival. As a result, and having heard the initial overview of your struggles, she says, "Let's get you a drink; it sounds like you need one."

Over the course of the next ninety minutes you end up having a great time. As well as you getting to vent about your problems (and see away a few drinks more quickly than you ordinarily would), the majority of the time is taken up by your single friend regaling the most extreme of her dating stories and sexual (mis)adventures since the last time you saw her. It's just the tonic you need: you laugh a lot and it makes you simultaneously forget about your troubles for a while and put them into perspective.

As it gets toward the witching hour for your friend, she suggests you and her have a little dance in a further effort to help you shake your stresses away. Your mood now lifted and you feeling entirely more relaxed, you agree.

There's sexy hip-hop beating out and the dancefloor is full of merry people, excited for both the weekend and the music, busting out their best moves. Fully conscious of the people and dancing around you for the first time, you briefly contemplate your own sexuality for a moment and decide to really work your body, especially when one of your favourite old-school hip-hop tracks comes on almost immediately after you've hit the dancefloor.

You and your friend dance away. You feel both the stress shaking away from you and bodies knocking into you, some accidentally and some deliberately. Those deliberately moving close to yours remind you how sexy you are, and, even though when you turn and see the people attempting to grind with you aren't as attractive as you might have hoped, the attention still lifts your mood and the slight bodily contact is both comforting and a little arousing.

Before you know it, though, your friend says she has to leave. Disappointed but accepting, you say goodbye. As she leaves, she asks what you're going to do now. You think briefly, whilst surveying the scene in the bar. After the week you've had, and, as you feel you've only just recovered and got started on the night out, you decide you're going to stay for a while.

Your friend walks out, leaving you free to make what you want of the night. You survey the scene a little more and decide to walk around and explore what else the bar has to offer. En route, from a distance you notice a guy carrying a tray of drinks walking through a door to another room. Curious, and with your sense of freedom and adventure restored by the fleeting interaction with your friend, you decide to follow the guy to see what else is behind the unmarked and generally innocuous door.

Although you have no particular expectations, what greets you as you descend the staircase immediately beyond the door is still a major surprise: The room, almost a paradisical oasis compared with the sweaty meat market of the floor above, is filled with what you quickly estimate to be about twenty-five men, drink in hand and deep in jovial conversation.

What you instantly notice most profoundly about the room is that all of the men are so solidly built that they appear as if they're busting out of the uniformed suits they're wearing. You realise you've stumbled into a private party of some sort of sports club and pause after taking just a few steps. But your feminine presence is like a tornado through the air which otherwise wreaks of testosterone and several of the men immediately spot you.

"Hi," one of the men says. Immediately, all the other men that hadn't yet noticed you halt their conversations and turn to look at you as well.

"Hi," you reply, initially unsure what else to say.

"Can we help you?" the man continues.

"I just came to have a look what's down here but I guess this is a private party?" you say, a little sheepishly.

"It is a private party but you're welcome to join us," the same man replies.

"I don't want to impose," you respond.

"You wouldn't be – in fact you'd make a nice change from this rabble!" he jokes.

After a brief pause, you decide you've got nothing to lose and say, "OK," and a friendly smile appears across your face. With that, you descend the rest of the staircase and towards the group.

"What can we get you?" the same guy asks you.

"The 'Screaming Orgasm' I just had was amazing so if I can get a 'Screaming Orgasm' down here as well then that would be great," you answer.

A few of the guys are both a little perplexed and have their interest in you piqued by this. The remainder know you're referring to a cocktail and grin.

"If it's a 'Screaming Orgasm' you want, it's a screaming orgasm you shall have," the same man replies. He turns to the single bar in what you have surmised by now is some sort of function room and looks toward the sole barman stood behind it to order for you but sees that he has heard and is already preparing your drink.

While you wait for your drink to arrive, you ask the group, who are all still fixated on you, "So, what's the deal with you guys? Are you some sort of club?"

"We play rugby. Our team's just finished a tour and we're having a bit of a knees-up," a different guy responds.

"Oh, rugby. It's not a sport I've ever played or even really watched. What can you teach me about it?" you say, your initial slight intimidation now gone and your confidence fully restored.

This open question rather flummoxes the men, some of whom look at each other and smirk, some of whom are clearly taken aback at your interest in the game and some of whom are just unsure where to begin to reply.

After a slight pause, one of the guys walks over to one side of the room, pulls out a rugby ball from a big bag that's sat there and says, "There's too much to teach in this forum so why don't we just give you a little taste of what it's like?" Without waiting for your reply, he throws the ball gently to you and you catch it. "There, you've received your first pass in rugby. You can now either run with the ball, kick it or throw it to one of us," he continues.

You look around at the men, who are all staring back at you. Instead of throwing the ball to one of them as they expect, you surprise them (particularly as you're wearing high heels) by running towards the far end of the bar. As you do so, a couple of the men head towards you, dip their upper bodies and put their arms around your thighs, one of their shoulders each making contact, to simulate a tackle. They grab you gently but sufficiently firmly enough to stop you in your tracks. As you do this, you get a feel for just how muscular the men are for the first time. Their shoulders and arms feel rock solid and the sensation of being penned in by the two of them from either side is arousing.

"Now you've had your first rugby tackle," the same guy says.

The two tacklers let you go and move away. You turn to the rest of the group, who are still staring intently at you, with a smile on your face. There's then a slightly awkward pause as everyone ponders what to do next.

"Have you ever heard of a scrum?" the same man eventually says.

"No, what's a scrum?" you enquire, intrigued.

"Again, rather than explain, why don't we provide you with a little demonstration? A scrum usually has sixteen players involved, eight from each side, but, given the size of the room and all the tables and chairs, I suggest we demonstrate this with just ten. Why don't you pick nine guys and you can be the tenth?" he finishes, turning a little and pointing his arm towards the other twenty-four men.

For the first time you get a chance to properly check out both the room and the men. The room is a big sleek affair, beautifully adorned with paintings on the walls, a fish tank in one corner, and solid wood tables and chairs – including one long table surrounded by sixteen chairs – each table separated by roughly five square metres.

The men are a smorgasbord of shapes, sizes and features. The only thing they have in common is the uniformed suits they are wearing and the giant muscles underneath, seemingly trying to burst out of them. Although plenty of them are not to your taste, as you scan the men you notice several who you find very attractive. Unbeknown to them, this is what you base your decision-making on.

"You," you say, pointing to one of them. "You," you repeat, pointing to another. You repeat this seven more times until the nine co-members of your scrum are all selected. Those selected take off their suit jackets, put down their drinks and move towards you. You watch them make their way, skipping your eyes between them, and the feel of their attractive presence coming towards you, looking at you and ultimately surrounding you is intoxicating.

Five of them assemble themselves in scrum formation a metre in front of you, three at the front and two behind. The three at the front stand in a line, the one in the middle puts his arms around the back of each of the men flanking him and then the men on each side put their nearest arm around the back of the man in the middle. The two behind also form a line and put their nearest arm around the back of each other before lowering their upper bodies and putting their heads between the gap beneath the interlocked arms and the lined up legs of the men in front to form a conjoined five-man unit.

The other team scrum formation complete, you feel one man move up against you on either side and put their arm around you in the same way as the other team. Having seen how the other team took up their formation, you likewise put your arms around these men. You then feel two men come up behind you, with one slotting his head through the gap between the man on your right's body and yours, and the other doing likewise on your left-hand side. The four men all lock in tightly against you and it slightly shocks you, the bulk of them pressing hard against you on three sides.

"Now, you crouch," one of the unselected men says. You see the three interlocked men at the front of the five opposite dip their upper bodies, leaving their shoulders and heads facing towards you at the height of your midriff.

You don't even get a chance to control your own crouch; the two men either side of you dip, and with you locked to them, are taken down with them. The ten of you are now stood crouched, the five of you facing off against the other five. Your head is barely a foot away from your opposite number and he's looking straight into your eyes.

"Hold," the same unselected man says, firmly this time as if he were a referee. You are then dragged towards the other five by your scrum-mates and feel your head and shoulders get locked into the opposite scrum team.

The ten of you have now formed a perfect scrum. You're all stood there, crouched and locked together, three sets of shoulders pushed up against the other three and two sets of men behind pushing up behind the front three. It's not comfortable but at the same time it feels good having so much masculinity pressed up against you and surrounding you. All you can see now are the men's bottom halves, heads and the floor. You notice for the first time the size of their leg muscles, which also seem to be trying to bust out of their suits, as well as the scent of the men you're locked together with, which you find strong but pleasant.

"Engage," shouts the same unselected man stood a few metres away. On this command, all nine other men start using their legs to push forward with their shoulders. Initially, there's little movement as the strength of the pushing results in something of a stalemate, the shoulders of each of the front three of each team pushed firmly against those of their opposite number. But eventually science prevails and you being scarcely half the size of the men surrounding you results in the scrum pushing your way, slowly at first as your teammates dig their feet in but exponentially more quickly as the momentum of the other team's superior strength overpowers yours.

The pushing causes all of your team to step back increasingly quickly (but still interlocked with the other team), but the combination of the increasing speed and you being in high heels causes you to lose your footing and the whole scrum ends up collapsing, with your team of five all falling backwards onto the floor and the other team of five all falling forwards on top of you.

Your fall is cushioned by your four muscle-bound teammates who are still intertwined with you such that you end up laid on top of them, one in particular being left stationed right underneath you. But you're immediately rather squashed by the weight of the men that fall on top of you and your team; you being at the centre sees one fall directly on top of you but you can still feel the weight of the others interlocked with that man pushing down on your sides. Again, it's somewhat uncomfortable, but at the same time you are deeply aroused by having nine muscle-bound men pressed up against and around you from all sides.

After a brief pause as you overcome the shock of the fall and settle into the situation in which you find yourself, you realise you're not the only one that has become aroused. You can feel something hard pressing up against both your bum and your groin. Although you are essentially paralysed and so can't initially move to check, you surmise from the feeling that the men laid directly on top of you ("Man 1") and underneath you ("Man 2") have erections, especially when you notice Man 1 is staring into your eyes.

The feeling of two erect penises pressed up against your groin and ass turns you on a little more. But, partly pretending to ignore these erections, you ask, a little cheekily, "Was that supposed to happen?" looking at Man 1, whose face is barely a couple of inches above yours, but partly talking to the entire scrum.

"Well, the idea is to drive forward while staying on your feet but sometimes the scrum does collapse," Man 1 says. He's completely oblivious to the fact that your question is a double-entendre.

"I wasn't talking about rugby," you reply, wrestling your right arm free from its paralysis, moving it down through the small gap between your bodies and gently caressing both of the bulges pressing into you through their trousers in turn as you do so.

You can see from Man 1's reaction that he's both shocked by this and enjoying it. He also looks a touch embarrassed at both his mistake and this happening surrounded by twenty-four other teammates, and clearly doesn't know how to reply. But after a slight pause he regains his composure and softly says, "Why do you think I positioned myself opposite you?"

There's a brief pause as you stare into each other's eyes. Then he moves his face ever so slowly towards yours and kisses you softly on the lips. He holds his lips pressed up against yours for just a couple of seconds and then withdraws his face back a couple of inches, holding your stare, as if to ask for your consent to engage in some debauchery with you with his mouth.

Deducing this, you validate his request by forcing your left arm free of its paralysis and joining it with your right arm down by your groin before using both to undo the button and zip at the top of his suit trousers, without breaking your gaze into his eyes. You then grope his package once more, this time with both hands and unencumbered by trousers. Man 2 can feel this happening right up above his groin and whispers into your right ear, "What about the rest of us?"

"I want all of you," you reply, loudly enough that the rest of the scrum can hear you but quietly enough that the unselected sixteen stood a few metres away, all watching on bemused, can't.

With that, you feel Man 2 start softly kissing your right ear and the back of your neck, whilst simultaneously slowly undoing the zip on the back of your dress. At the same time, Man 1 starts softly kissing the left side of the front of your neck and your shoulder as he pulls down the strap on your dress.

The next thing you notice is the other four men at the front of the scrum – the one on the right and the one on the left of you and the one on the right and left of the team opposite ("Man 3", "Man 4", "Man 5" and "Man 6") – break their arms free and start gently stroking parts of your body with their newly-freed hands too, initially the sides of your upper body and then all over your legs, abdomen and back.

There isn't much left of you for the remaining three men at the back of the scrum ("Man 7", "Man 8" and "Man 9") to get to but that doesn't stop them from trying; you can't tell it's them from your sandwiched position but their hands too start touching the scarce parts of your body that aren't otherwise engaged – your feet, ankles and other gaps that appear as the other men's hands and lips move around your body.

The feel of nine men's hands and lips, as well as their breath, all over your body feels fantastic and you start to let out the occasional gasp of breath in indication of your enjoyment. This soft but ubiquitous stimulation, combined with the feel of nine muscular bodies (and two erections), still pressed up against you from every direction, causes your vagina to start flooding.

As if they can smell the arrival of the flood, Man 1 and Man 2 start to pull down your dress from both the front and back, with their kissing of your soft skin following it. Man 3, Man 4, Man 5 and Man 6 adjust their hand positions accordingly – lower down your legs and to the top of your back and neck. Man 7, Man 8 and Man 9 adjust where they stroke you as a result.

As you feel yourself start to be undressed in earnest, you decide you want to unclothe those around you as well so that you can feel their skin and bodies directly against yours. You start with the easiest, unbuttoning the shirt of Man 1 and then peeling both this and his already-undone trousers off to reveal his muscle-bound physique for the first time. Then you reach behind to unbutton and unzip the trousers and, as best you can, shirt of Man 2. Then you move on to Man 3 and Man 4, above you on either side, first unbuttoning and then peeling off their shirts, before doing likewise with their trousers, which you notice also have bulges poking through them in your direction.

Looking around as much as your squashed position allows, you conclude that you can also reach Man 7 and Man 8's trousers so you also reach to undo these. You can't reach to pull them down but again you see bulges facing back at you through their now-revealed boxer shorts. Whilst doing your best to undress as many of the scrum as possible, Man 2 has also removed your bra and the men closest to you are now fondling and kissing your breasts, as well as continuing to stroke and kiss the rest of you as best they can.

After a few minutes of this, Man 1 decides he wants more. He lifts up the bottom of your dress as well so that it's all gathered around your midriff and your thong is fully visible for the first time. He lifts his erection off you slightly and replaces it against your groin with his hand. You feel the direct stimulation of your pussy for the first time and it's just what you want by this stage. You let out a moan as you feel Man 1's fingers slide over your clitoris for the first time.

"Like that, do you?" he says quietly into your ear, as he continues to slide his fingers over your now-drenched thong.

"Yes," you quietly reply.

"Maybe we should take off this wet little thong?" he continues.

"Yeah, take it off," you reply.

Man 1 slides off your thong to reveal your soaking wet pussy for the first time. Although the fragrance of it was already pervading from within your thong, the removal of your underwear only serves to unleash it on those around you. Inhaling it, Man 2 still firmly planted underneath you and with his erection still poking into your backside, whispers in your ear, "Your pussy smells so good – like it needs some cock inside it."

"Oh yeah? Let's give it what it needs then," you respond breathlessly, now so turned on from all the stimulation of having the men around you – and their words, lips, breath, hands, scent, muscles and erections – as well as being in the knowledge that, even though you can't see them through the melee of men surrounding you, there's a crowd watching the show unfolding in front of them with you its star.

Hearing this, Man 1 removes the hand that's been continuing to stroke your pussy and uses it to pull down his boxer shorts. The next thing you feel is his rock-hard penis enter you. You let out a gasp as you feel yourself being penetrated. It feels glorious. Man 1 starts slowly thrusting in and out of you, his body still pressed on top of yours. Meanwhile, Man 2 is continuing to kiss and stroke you from underneath and the rest of the scrum continue using their hands to stroke the rest of your body. The multiple stimulation persists and it feels thrilling.

After a few minutes of this, Man 2, seemingly now de facto controller of proceedings, whispers, "How would you like another cock inside of you?" in your ear.

"Oh yeah," you half-say, half-pant.

Another erect penis appears right above your eyes and lands on your lips. Man 6 has removed his clothing, shuffled up towards you and contorted his body so as to be able to dangle his ample package in your direction. You open your mouth and ingest as much of it as you can while pressed between all these men. Knowing that your movement is restricted, Man 6 starts slowly and gently thrusting his cock backwards and forwards in your mouth. You do your best to start sucking on it as it moves inside you. Man 6 lets out a groan of pleasure as you do so.

"You like having two dicks in you?" Man 2 enquires into your right ear, while continuing to fondle and kiss you from underneath.

"Mmm," you reply, unable to speak with your mouth full of Man 6's cock.

"How would you like one in your ass as well?" Man 2 then asks.

"Mmm," you again reply, before momentarily opening your mouth from around Man 6's cock to say. "Yeah, I want dick in my ass as well," to make it clear that the "Mmm" means you definitely want it, right now, before replacing your mouth around Man 6's dick.

Little do you know it but some of your sexual juices have been seeping out of your pussy and down on to Man 2 below as Man 1 has been thrusting in and out of you.

With the green light to penetrate your ass, Man 2 gathers some of these juices with his fingers, wipes them over both his hard cock and the opening of your ass and uses it as a lubricant to smooth his entrance into you.

You let out another "Mmm", louder this time, as you feel him enter you. He begins thrusting in and out of your ass, to join the two dicks of Man 1 and Man 6 thrusting into your vagina and mouth. Man 2 then grabs your breasts with his hands from behind you to both stimulate them and use them to lever his thrusting. The other men again adjust their stroking of you, moving their hands to the areas they can get to between the three men with their dicks in you.

Man 1 and Man 2 proceed to speed up and increase the force of their thrusting, and start letting out grunts as they do so, right in your ears. You start to let out sporadic moans of pleasure, most of which are muffled by the cock in your mouth, as the feeling of being dominated by all these men, and having three of them fill your orifices, leaves you in heaven.

But Man 2 decides this isn't enough penis for you to be dealing with; he asks, "Want some more cock?"

"Mmm," you once again reply. While continuing to fuck your ass, Man 2 proceeds to remove his hands from your breasts, grab each of your hands with them, manoeuvre your hands towards the erections of Man 7 and Man 8 situated nearby, and then clasp them around Man 7 and Man 8's shafts. Feeling the two new erections in your hands, you realise you're expected to handle these as well, all while taking the three dicks that are already thrusting into you. You do your best to start jerking Man 7 and Man 8 off, despite being encumbered by the shaking of the triple fucking you're getting and the semi-paralysis of having nine muscular men's physiques squashed up against you from all directions.

You're now pleasuring five men at once, made clear by the intermittent groans and grunts you can hear coming from all angles. You're having the time of your life; having all your holes filled feels incredible, as does knowing that you're concurrently giving pleasure to so many men at once. You almost wish you had more orifices that the rest of the men could penetrate. You synchronously pleasuring the five men at once whilst being stroked by the remaining four continues for a few minutes and you don't want it to stop. But Man 2 then decides it's about time that, to accede to your earlier statement that you want all the men, there should be a switch in roles. "Want some fresh cock inside you?" he asks.

"Mmm," you once again reply, still sucking on Man 6's solid cock as you do so.

With your agreement, he gently pushes the arms of Man 1, Man 6, Man 7 and Man 8 so as to make it clear it's time for them to exit your vagina, mouth and hands, and pulls on the arms of Man 3, Man 4, Man 5 and Man 9 to make it clear that they should take Man 1, Man 6, Man 7 and Man 8's positions. Some ungainly shuffling follows to enable the necessary switching amidst the scrum. Man 2 continues to fuck your ass the whole time, though, keen to ensure there's not a complete let up in your stimulation.

After a few seconds you see Man 9 shuffle on top of you and feel him enter your vagina. His erect penis is bigger than Man 1's and you feel it deep inside you right from the start, letting out a moan as it completely fills you.

Next, Man 4's hard cock appears above your mouth, which you open to allow it in, then close around it and begin sucking. Then you once again feel Man 2's hands guide you, this time to Man 3 and Man 5's hard cocks, which are now either side of you, more or less where Man 7 and Man 8's were moments before.

With Man 2's help, you clasp Man 3 and Man 5's shafts and begin tugging them as best you can. With Man 2 continuing to thrust into your ass from underneath, Man 9's big, hard penis starts to thrust into your vagina. As if to make up for lost time while you were pleasuring the other men, he very quickly increases the speed and intensity of his thrusting. You feel your vagina and ass completely filled and the mutual thrusting into them feels wonderful. You let out regular moans right into Man 4's cock, which you're doing your best to suck amidst the fucking by Man 2 and Man 9 and tossing off of Man 3 and Man 5. You hear all five men groan and grunt back at you as you simultaneously pleasure them all.

Matters continue like this for some time before Man 2 again decides it's time to switch things up, even though you're clearly absolutely in your element and all nine men have now had the delight of you pleasuring them via either your hands, mouth, vagina or ass.

He again gently pushes Man 9, Man 3 and Man 5 away. But this time, instead of continuing to thrust into your ass and pulling other men towards you, you are surprised when he pushes the other men right off you and stops thrusting.

Still in your ass, he rolls you over so your body hits the floor for the first time, he rolls with you and on top of you, removes your dress that's been rolled up around your midriff all this time, and then starts thrusting into your ass again, more forcefully now he has more freedom to do so and in the knowledge that you've had no issue with his cock fucking your ass thus far. "Your tight ass feels so good," he whispers in your ear as he does so.

After forcefully sodomising you on the floor like this for a minute or so, he stops and proceeds to slowly lift you up, standing up himself in the process, cock still in your ass, carries you over to the long table, drapes you over it so your feet are touching the floor and your upper body is laid flat on the table, his hands pressing down on your shoulders, and then begins thrusting into your ass once again, even more forcefully this time.

At this point, you notice for the first time the crowd of unselected men all staring at you. They've all been delighting in watching you getting gang-banged – albeit are rather jealous that they're not part of it – and are just as turned on by watching you get pummelled in the ass over the table by Man 2. Man 2 pounds your ass like this for another couple of minutes, asking, "You like this?" as he does so when he sees that you've spotted the unselected men watching you.

"Oh yeah," you reply, looking at the unselected men as you do so, as if saying the words partly for them as well as for Man 2. Although you're only being fucked by one guy right now, the manner in which he's dealing with you leaves you feeling just as dominated as when you were pleasuring five and surrounded by nine.

Then, out of nowhere, Man 2 halts his pounding of your ass and withdraws from it. He moves round and joins you on the table, lifts your upper body up slightly and positions himself under it so that his cock is facing your mouth and his face is a few centimetres from your pussy. He beckons Man 3 towards the two of you with his hands. You then feel Man 2's tongue start sliding over your pussy for the first time and Man 3's hard cock enter your vagina and start thrusting into you, seconds apart.

The combination of having your pussy licked and being fucked from behind feels glorious, and you once again start moaning with pleasure. You decide you should reciprocate the pleasure Man 2 is giving you and take his cock, fresh from your ass, in your mouth, spitting on it and wiping the saliva all over it with a quick couple of jerks before you do so as if to both clean it and establish just how hard it is.

The other seven members of the scrum then move over to you and once again start fondling your body with their hands as you're simultaneously pleasured by Man 2 and Man 3. As they move towards you, you can see out of the corner of your eyes that the other seven are still fully erect and you reach your spare hands out either side of the table to grab two of their erections, Man 1 and Man 6's. From this position, your arms free, you're able to do a better job of jerking them off.

The ten of you pleasuring and/or being pleasured, you at the centre of it, is a seriously arousing sight and the unselected men are thoroughly enjoying the show unfolding before them – some so much that they're desperate to start masturbating (or ideally join in), although they restrain themselves.

Man 3 spends a few minutes pounding your vagina but then, out of nowhere, withdraws from your vagina. "I wanna fuck your ass," he says and immediately inserts his rock-hard dick, covered in your juices, into your ass instead. You continue sucking Man 2 and tossing off Man 1 and Man 6 as Man 2 licks you out and Man 3 thrusts into your ass. There are moans and groans aplenty from all of the pleasure being dished out.

This continues for some time before, again out of the blue, Man 3 withdraws from your ass when he feels himself getting close to orgasm. Before you know it, he's replaced by Man 7, who inserts his cock into your vagina and starts pummelling you. "Your pussy feels so good," he says.

After a few minutes of Man 7 fucking your vagina, he then repeats the actions of Man 3 by exiting your vagina and sliding his cock, also now covered in your juices, into your ass, which is now used to having penis thrusting in and out of it.

After a few minutes of riding your tight ass, he too can feel himself getting close to orgasm and withdraws. He's immediately replaced by Man 8 who repeats what he's witnessed Man 7 and Man 3 do to you, first roughly fucking your vagina and then following suit with your ass.

This pattern continues until all the other members of the scrum except Man 2 have taken their turns in your vagina and ass, all while Man 2 continues to lick your pussy. Some of the men opt to spit on your ass before entering it to add some lubricant to smooth their entry into you. Each time, the remainder of the men rotate duties in your mouth or hands or stroking your silky soft skin.

Once all of the men except Man 2 have had their way with you in both your vagina and ass, Man 2 lifts you up off his face, flips you 180 degrees with his strong arms so you have your ass to his face. He then turns himself 180 degrees until he's back directly underneath you, you both fully on top of the table at one end. He plunges his cock back into your ass, clasps your left breast with his left hand once again and beckons two of the other men, Man 1 and Man 9, toward the two of you with his right.

Man 1 mounts the table and places himself on top of you, his cock dangling in your face and his mouth aligned with your pussy. He starts to slide his tongue over your pussy and you reciprocate on his cock with your mouth.

The sandwich is then joined by Man 9's mighty penis, which he slides into your vagina. Man 4 and Man 7 move up alongside the table and Man 2 once again takes your hands and moves them until they have Man 4 and Man 7's erections clasped by them.

Man 9 starts thrusting his big dick in and out of your vagina and Man 2 does likewise in your ass. Man 1 slides his tongue over your pussy, especially your clitoris, while you suck his dick and jerk off Man 4 and Man 7. Having three dicks inside you and two in your hands, all now throbbing, once again feels thrilling. But this time, with the addition of Man 1's tongue on your pussy, it feels out of this world.

As Man 2's cock thrusts into your ass, Man 9's mighty penis thrusts hard into your vagina and Man 1's tongue caresses your clitoris and around, you moan repeatedly, louder and louder with each thrust and lick, right into Man 1's dick.

You feel Man 4 and Man 7 get even harder in your hands. All of the cocks of the five men you're concurrently pleasuring are so hard and throbbing now it's clear they could explode at any moment. But you're so lost in your own ecstasy that it still catches you by surprise when Man 1 is sent over the edge by the vibration of your increasingly loud moaning into his cock and starts ejaculating into your mouth, accompanying it with a roar of pleasure. Already so close to climax yourself, this is enough to tip you over the edge and you let out an almighty scream as you have an equally almighty orgasm.

Your almighty scream, the sight and feel of you climaxing, and the tensing of your body and hands around their cocks is enough to send Man 9, Man 2, Man 4 and Man 7 over the edge. You're showered in their semen, your vagina and ass flooded with Man 9 and Man 2's loads firing into you and Man 4 and Man 7's loads squirting all over your arms, sides and even your face and breasts, to accompany the mouthful of Man 1's cum that has continued to spurt into your mouth while you climax. Your eyes roll through your head and it feels like the ecstasy flowing through your body carries on for longer than you've ever felt before.

Eventually, your orgasm subsides and you return to full consciousness to find Man 1 removing himself from on top of you, and then Man 9 withdrawing himself from your vagina. You realise your hands are still tightly clasped around Man 4 and Man 7's still hard but no longer throbbing dicks and release them.

But Man 2 goes nowhere, leaving his softening cock in your ass and keeping his arms wrapped around you to hold you in place. Although somewhat overwhelmed from the workout you've been given, and still in a post-orgasmic haze, you realise that there are still four members of the scrum that haven't had the ultimate finish that the rest of you have and you decide that you want to deliver this for them.

They desperately want the same and have already crowded around you. "Who wants me first?" you say, looking around at the four men as you do so. Quick as a flash, Man 5 inserts himself in your vagina, still flooded with the majority of Man 9's spunk, as well as your juices, and begins thrusting hard in and out of you. "I wanna cum in your pussy," he says, looking straight into your eyes as he does so.

"Do it. Cum in my pussy," you reply, looking straight back at him.

He continues to fuck you, more furiously after you say this, even more aroused by your words than he already was by you. As Man 5 delights in fucking you, Man 2 grabs your face and turns it towards Man 6, who's stationed to your right, his erect penis facing right at you. You grab it with your right hand and start stroking it, looking into his eyes as you do so. Keeping his gaze with yours, you ask him, "Where do you want to cum?"

"On your tits," he replies.

"Do it. Cum all over my tits," you say, almost demanding it, tugging at his cock more firmly as you do so.

As you continue to jerk Man 6 off and take Man 5's pounding of your vagina, Man 2 again turns your head, this time to your left where Man 8 is waiting, his hard cock once again staring directly at you. Once again, you grab his erection, begin stroking it, look him in the eyes and ask him, "Where do you want to cum?"

"On your face," he replies.

"Do it. Cum all over my face," you say, again tugging his cock more firmly as you do so.

Now jerking both Man 6 and Man 8 off, while being fucked by Man 5, Man 2 turns your head once again, this time further to the left where Man 3 is waiting, his hard penis again staring at you. Man 3 doesn't wait for you to say anything; instead he simply says, "Open wide." And thrusts his erection towards your mouth. You duly oblige, opening your mouth and taking his member into it as best you can with no free hands to assist you and while being shaken from the pummelling you're getting from Man 5. Man 2 pushes your head back and forth so as to force your mouth to slide up and down Man 3's shaft. You eventually get a good grip on Man 3's dick with your mouth and begin sucking it, forcefully from the get-go.

In next to no time you've gone from simultaneously pleasuring five men to orgasm, whilst enjoying your own incredible orgasm, to simultaneously pleasuring another four men. After everything that's gone before, and with the extra arousal for these four men of seeing you handle these four cocks all at once while drenched in semen, and hearing your dirty talk, acquiescing to their desires, as you look them in the eye, it doesn't take long before you feel all of their cocks start throbbing to the edge of orgasm in your vagina, mouth and hands. Feeling this, you do your best to tug and suck Man 6, Man 8 and Man 3 even more frenetically, and even, in the case of Man 5, tighten your vagina around his throbbing cock.

Then follows the inevitable carnage as the all-encompassing stimulation you're giving these men becomes too great and they climax, all accompanied by prolonged groans. Once again, you're flooded with semen – a second load in your vagina and mouth, as well as one sprayed all over your breasts and one showering across your eyes, nose, cheeks, forehead and ears. You keep working these men's cocks until you're sure they have completely finished orgasming and every last drop of cum has ejaculated from them.

Eventually, the four men return to earth and start to withdraw and untangle themselves from you. There's then a delay for several seconds as you first look down at yourself and then around at the men, all twenty-five of them except for Man 2 now standing around looking at you. For them, you're a sight to behold and they're transfixed.

You're not quite sure what to do as you can feel cum virtually everywhere, inside and out, and you worry somewhat as to what might happen to it with any movement. But then you decide that you don't care; you're already so drenched and feeling epic from having just been gang-banged by nine attractive men – putting on a phenomenal show in the process for sixteen others – and having spent a couple of hours giving and receiving the most incredible amount of intense pleasure. So you lift yourself off Man 2, sit up on the edge of the table and then stand up (as best you're able after the pounding you've just taken), your eyes looking around at the group as you do so.

The spunk slides down your skin and starts dripping out of your vagina and ass. Keen to break the awkward silence, you ignore it and, with a smile, you say, "Well, I certainly got the *Screaming Orgasm* I asked for!"